SEAL SEC
GF

AUTHOR
SUSIE MCIVER

Copyright © 2023 by Susie McIver

All rights reserved.

No part of this publication may be reproduced, distributed, or transmitted in

any form or by any means, including photocopying, recording, or other electronic or mechanical methods, without the prior written permission of

the publisher, except as permitted by U.S. copyright law. For permission request, contact Susie McIver susie.mciver@yahoo.com

Book Cover by Amanda Walker

❀ Created with Vellum

1
GILLY

I cried like a baby in the movie theatre. My blind date kept handing me more Kleenex tissues because the lady behind him passed them to him as fast as if trying to stop water from a spout. She made a noise for me to shut up. All of the people around me, wanted me to be quiet. But I could not stop crying. I had so many people silencing me, I couldn't even begin to tell you how many there were. I could tell my blind date was exasperated with me. But he was the one who picked the movie, so it was all on him.

Now everyone knows why I do not watch sad movies. I cried while watching them or got horrible headaches from trying not to cry. Plus, the tragic film would make me sad for an entire week. Who dies in a romance for crying out loud? I only like happily ever after romance movies, not that I watch much television. I enjoy reading if I have extra time, but I am always busy.

I turned to the guy who was my blind date. He was very handsome in an outdoor strong looking way. He watched me closely, waiting to see if I needed another kleenex.

"Look, I am ready to leave. I will only cry more, thinking about how this movie will end. So far, I'm pretty sure I know the ending."

"Then why did your grandma tell mine that you love sad movies? Hell, your grandma picked out the movie."

"My grandma died last year. How long have you had this information?" I asked, walking out of the theater. "Besides, I do not watch movies. Why would people say that actors and sports players are heroes? My father was a hero. He died fighting overseas." We stopped in the lobby, and he looked at me, and I looked at him. Damn, I felt that feeling down in my core again, if you know what I mean. When I first laid eyes on him, I felt it. I needed to pull my panties away from me. They were already sticky. He smelled so good. I wanted to tase him.

He pulled out his paper, shaking his head as he read it. "Is your name Gilda Staples? You live at three hundred Fifth Avenue. That's where the taxi took me, so I have the right address."

I sucked on my bottom lip to keep myself from chuckling. *His eyes are beautiful. Keep him.* I chuckled again as that thought popped into my head. "No, my name is Gillian Marshall. I live at three hundred Sixth Avenue. It would seem you picked up the wrong woman."

I couldn't help it. I burst into laughter. At first, he looked at me like I was crazy, but I saw the laughter in those beautiful eyes. I might add his beautiful stormy gray eyes, I felt them suck me closer to him. Then I looked at him. Damn, this guy was hot. He was about six foot two. His dark hair fell onto his forehead. I reached up and moved it to the side. *Stop it right now, Gilly. You do not touch him again. He is not yours!*

His eyes narrowed when he looked at me. "Sorry," I said,

stepping back.

"Then why did you go out with me if you aren't my blind date?"

"Because my blind date's name is Grayson, I assumed you were him when you introduced yourself as Grayson. I figured you were just early."

"Are you telling me he has the same last name as mine?"

"I didn't pay any attention to his last name. Sorry."

"How can this happen?" He looked at me. I still had a grin on my face. I watched as his eyes lit up, and then he started laughing. "Damn, I need to explain what happened to the other woman. I'm sure my grandmother will hear about this from her grandmother."

"Good luck with the other woman. I held out my hand. He put his hand into mine. Heat ran over my body, I tried to block it out. "It was nice meeting you, Grayson."

"Call me Gray. All my friends do. It was nice meeting you too. So, you don't like movies?"

"I watch some, but never this kind. Goodbye."

"Let me take you home." We were on the sidewalk by now.

"I think you better explain to Gilda what happened, or your grandma will let you know how unhappy she is."

Gray nodded, and I started to walk away. He didn't let go of my hand. I turned, and his mouth landed on mine. I knew I should have made him stop, but my arms wrapped around him, they went inside his jacket and gave him a body hug. It wasn't like any kiss I'd ever had. When he raised his head, I swayed. His lips touched mine again, and I took a step back. My body almost tipped to the side. His arm reached out and held on until I got my balance.

I turned and kept walking. I had to get away from this hot-as-hell man. He'd have me a hot mess if I didn't leave. I shook my head. I couldn't believe the man I wanted to go to bed with was my wrong date. I chuckled all the way home. When I got there, a man was sitting on my steps.

"Is your name Grayson?"

"Yes, I wondered if you were standing me up."

I chuckled as I explained what had happened. I couldn't help but compare this Grayson to my other Grayson. *Well, actually, he's not mine. But I can dream. Maybe he'll come by and see me sometime?* The wrong blind date had eyes so gray that they almost looked silver. His hair was thick, and the color was as dark as a raven's wings. His scent would stay with me for many nights. *There I go again, getting my panties in a mess.*

Okay, Gilly, stop right now. He was the wrong date, which is how you will think of him. I wondered how he and his real date were getting along. *That is a chapter in my life that I will close. Maybe I won't. He may come back to see me. I can hope.*

"Have you had dinner yet?"

I have to stop thinking about the other Grayson.

I shook my head, determined to enjoy the rest of my evening. So, what if this guy wasn't six-two with beautiful eyes? He was cute. His eyes were a lovely hazel. So, what if my panties didn't get wet or he didn't disrupt my breathing pattern? "No, I haven't eaten. I would love to go to dinner with you. How about a steak? We have a steak house around the block. We can walk."

"Wonderful, we might make this a memorable night after all. I have to tell you, though, I'm a vegetarian."

"Oh, I can have a chicken salad, that way, you don't have to watch me eat my medium-rare steak."

"Thank you. A lot of women don't care if they cut into the meat while I'm there trying not to watch."

My mind drifted to my wrong date, wondering what he had for dinner.

2

GRAYSON

I wanted to take her bottom lip and suck on it like she was doing. Damn, she was hot. I wondered why she needed a blind date. She must have had the same problem I had with my grandma, who always tried setting me up. Except her grandmother passed away. It must be her friends who set her up. I agreed to go this time, and look where that got me. I had to let my beautiful prize go to her real blind date.

I was harder than hell as I looked into those laughing green eyes as she sucked on that plump bottom lip. I knew if she looked down, she would see I was hard. Her hair looked like honey-colored silk. It was thick and wavy. I wanted to dig my fingers into it while she lay naked beneath me.

When she moved my hair off my forehead, I almost took those fingers and nibbled on them. I couldn't stop taking that kiss for anything. Her soft lips called to me, and they melted when they touched mine. I ached to touch her entire body. I had to force myself not to taste her neck. She fit me perfectly. *I'll visit her tomorrow and see if she'll have dinner with me.*

Alright, Gray, you can stop daydreaming and see if your date is waiting for you. I know grandma will hear about this. Then what will she say? She will most likely laugh.

I took a taxi to the correct address this time and knocked on the door. An angry woman answered. "Are you my blind date?" she demanded.

"Yes, I'm sorry I'm late," I explained to her what had happened. She laughed, but I noticed it didn't reach her eyes, which weren't emerald or green. But they were a soft brown. "That must have been uncomfortable."

"She laughed it off. I did the same. It's good that she didn't care for the movie, or I would have been later than I am."

"Hmm, I loved that movie. I was so looking forward to seeing it again."

I decided not to take the hint that she wanted to see the movie again. "I heard there is a great steak house not far from here. Why don't we go there for dinner?"

"I know where it is, but I hoped to cook you dinner. I don't particularly like eating other people's food. Please come in. I've already got the salad ready. I'll put the rest of the dinner in the oven. It won't take no time to cook."

What have I gotten myself into?

"Grayson, please make yourself comfortable; you can sit right here," she said, pointing to the head of the table. "I'll make the dressing. I'm making chicken parmesan for our dinner. I didn't realize my grandmother would know my taste in men. I have to be honest with you, I don't sleep with a man on the first date, but I will make an exception with you." She giggled, and I stopped breathing.

NO! My mind shouted. Hell no! "I'm flattered that you would make me an exception. But I wouldn't sleep with a woman I just met." *I would have slept with Gilly.* "I do not sleep with someone just because I'm dating her. I have to know her before we sleep together."

"Oh, I'm so embarrassed. You must think I'm so forward. Please forgive me."

"No, I don't think that at all." She put the salad in front of me before moving to the other end of the table. *Someone was angry.* I could tell by the way she held herself and the sound my salad plate made hitting the table. *Damn, there is nothing worse than an angry woman.*

I decided to start a conversation to get rid of the uncomfortable silence. I took a bite of the salad and couldn't help the slight cough as I gasped for breath. The salad dressing was lemon and black pepper. I mean pure lemon and lots of black pepper. I tried to pick through the lettuce that looked like it wasn't covered in the dressing and pepper, but the lid must have come off the lemon bottle because my salad was soaked in it. The black pepper was on so heavy I coughed again. I took a drink of water with each bite. When I ran out of that, I took a sip of the wine she poured me and started coughing.

"Are you alright?"

"Yes, excuse me, it went down the wrong side," I said, trying to clear my throat. *What the hell kind of wine is this? I don't think it is wine.* "What kind of wine is this?" I asked, trying to clear my throat.

"Oh, it's not wine. I don't believe in any alcoholic beverage. I served you apple cider vinegar with the mother. It is healthy for you to drink. I always drink it with my dinner."

"Oh." I didn't know what else to say. "Could I please get more water?"

"Yes, I'll get it for you right now. How do you like the salad? It's my very own dressing recipe. The chicken is also my recipe. I just put a little twist on the parmesan recipe. I'm thinking about writing a cookbook."

"Oh, I'm sure you will get good reviews on it." What's one little lie? I wanted to give her confidence. Maybe she hadn't changed the parmesan too much.

"Thank you. I'll check to see if the chicken is ready."

Is she going to get my water? I guess I'll get it myself. Wait, didn't she just put that in the oven? I got up and went into the kitchen to get some more water. I stopped in the doorway. The woman was a hoarder. There was no available spot in the kitchen. I must have been quiet because it was apparent, she didn't hear me. Her kitchen was filthy. There was garbage everywhere. Dirty dishes were everywhere. She didn't turn around from her task. She took a container from the microwave and poured more vinegar into it. I turned and left before she saw me and returned to the dining room. I chewed my bottom lip, wondering how to get out of eating more of her food.

"It's ready. Here you go," she put a large plate of food in front of me. It was a frigging platter. I knew my eyes bulged, but I couldn't help it. The vegetables were still frozen. I could see the freezer burn on them. I looked at her to see if she was playing a prank on me. I saw a woman with a look that waited for me to say something.

"It looks delicious."

"Thank you. I know you will love it. This is one of my best recipes."

Okay, Gray, you can at least take a few bites. That won't kill you. When I looked up, she waited for me to take the first bite. I didn't know where to take my first bite. I cut a piece of something, I wasn't sure what it was, but I didn't want to eat any chicken because of salmonella. I hoped she couldn't see the small bite on my fork. I quickly popped it into my mouth. I almost choked. The vinegar was so strong. I forced myself to swallow. I knew my eyes must have been watering. I reached for my glass of water, and it was empty. "May I have more water, please?"

"Yes, I'll get it. How is your dinner?"

"It's delicious."

"Thank you."

I watched as she took a bite and then another. Was she going to get my water? I got my glass and stood up.

"Where are you going?"

"To get some water."

"I said I would get it. Here, give it to me."

She jerked the glass out of my hand. I worked fast and dumped most of my food in a container in the corner of the room. The more I looked around, I noticed sheets covered stuff everywhere. There was a walkway from the door to the dining room. How did I not see this before?

"Here you go."

"Thank you, I had a call, and I'm sorry, but I have to leave. My parents are here from out of state and decided to drop in and are now at my house." *What's one lie?*

"That is so rude. Why don't you tell your parents to leave, and you will see them another time? After all, you already screwed up my day. Are you going to make it worse?"

"I'm sorry. I would never treat my parents like that," I stood up and smiled. "Thank you for a wonderful dinner. Good luck with your cookbook." She was frowning. My grandma would get an ear full, and I didn't care.

"Okay, why don't you call me, and we can do something? Maybe it'll be better than this date."

"I'm going to be out of town for a few months, maybe when I return. I'm always so busy." I was going to the front door when she grabbed my hand. The next thing I knew, she put my hand over her boob.

"Can you feel my heart beating for you?"

To say I was surprised would be almost correct. I had a panic moment. I know that's crazy, but this entire day was crazy—all except when I gazed into the emerald, green eyes of my wrong date and my lips touched hers.

"I loved what little time we had together. Thank you," Gilda raised her face to mine and closed her eyes. I kissed her cheek and got the hell out of there. When I got outside, I took a deep breath of clean air. This was the strangest day I've ever had in my twenty-four years here on earth.

3

GRAY

It'd been eight years since I met Gilly. There'd been a lot of women since that day. My entire life changed that night when I got home. My mom called me and said she needed me to come home. My dad had been taken to the hospital. I called a doctor friend who worked at the hospital in the town where I grew up. First, I called the airport and got a ticket home. Then I called Jack Johnson, my friend. As soon as he answered, he knew why I was calling.

"Gray, your dad isn't doing good. I'm sorry to tell you this, but I'm unsure if he will make it. I saw your family in the waiting room. I told them we were doing everything to save him. Pray, Gray, that's what we need now."

I prayed all the way home. My mom was in ICU with my dad when I arrived. When she saw me, she threw herself into my arms.

"He made it through the surgery," she whispered so Dad couldn't hear. "Now we have to pray he lives. I saw Jack. He said he talked to you. What did he say?"

"He told me to pray. Dad is strong. I know he doesn't

look like it now with all of these wires hooked up to him, but he is. He's going to make it."

My dad lived two months after. He came through, but his heart wasn't strong enough to keep him alive. We took him home, and that's where he died. We talked so much during those two months. We laughed when I told him about my wrong date. He looked sad. I knew he thought I should have gone back and talked to Gilly. And that was what I had planned on doing. But life happens.

I've thought about her many times over the last eight years. My dad was a Navy Seal. I always wanted to be a Seal. My brother Hutch is a Navy Seal. He joined right out of college. I hadn't signed up yet because my mom didn't want me to join the Seals.

When I graduated from college, I moved to the Silicon Valley in California and worked for a High-Tech company. I made a lot of money. I saved it all because my house was paid for and furnished. The company supplied all of that. I never returned to work in the bay area after my dad had his heart attack.

I stayed with my dad. He told me to join the Seals and live life as I wanted. We had long conversations. I wasn't going to leave and miss having a conversation with him. I wanted to spend every moment with him that I could. A couple of my college buddies packed my belongings and brought them to me in Cedar Falls, Oregon. I told them what I planned to do, and they both decided they wanted to join the Seals when I did.

"Here I am eight years later. I left the Seals and worked with my brother and some of our buddies, doing rescue missions. We do a lot of rescues at sea. People get into trouble thinking they can handle their yacht, and a storm comes up out of nowhere, and their boats start sinking. The ocean is vast. Sometimes we can't find them in time. All of us take it very hard if that happens.

This job was deadly if you didn't know what you were doing. That's why my brother was worried about me joining. I'm thirty-four, and he's thirty-six, but he still tries to be my big brother. He said our mom told him she wanted me to settle down and marry. We both laughed over that. Mom has been after both of us to get married. Six months after my dad died, my sister married my friend, Jack. They have three girls, and Jenny is pregnant again. Her having grandkids for mom has kept her off our back.

My brother Hutch looked at me, "Damn, this water is rough. Do you think there are any survivors on the oil rig?"

"If there is, I hope we find them fast. The caller said the rig was being inspected when the storm came up, and there was a fire."

"Listen, Gray. I know this is your specialty, but Mom would kill me if anything happened to you."

"Mom knows how careful I am. So, I don't want you to worry."

The large Navy ship made a deep dip as a giant wave hit us. We bought this vessel from the Navy when they would have to dock it for good. When you have friends in high places, that's what happens. You get to pick your vessel. We did all the maintenance and ensured it was always ready to go out in an emergency.

"I see it!" Gabe Steller shouted.

I ran up top. I could see the fire; all I could think of were burned bodies. I've seen it before when I had to rescue people from a rig on fire. Sweat broke out all over my body.

My brother shook his head. "We're going to abort this rescue. We all agreed that we would abort if it were too dangerous, and I'm the one that calls it. Let's get the hell out of here."

"Hutch, we can't. They might all be alive waiting for us."

"This isn't going to happen. It's too dangerous. I don't want you anywhere on that rig."

I threw my hands in the air. I was ready to throttle my brother. Sometimes he still treated me like his little brother. "Hutch, I can do it. Gabe will be with me. We are all dressed up and ready to go. Come on, Gabe, let's do this." We climbed inside the cage, and Hutch lowered us to the burning platform. The fire was on the other side. We needed to hurry. When it dangled over the offshore platform, I opened the cage door, and we jumped out.

"Can you hear me?" Hutch asked.

I waved my hand to let him know I heard him. We ran to the door and opened it. Damn, it was hot inside. "Stay close to me," I said to Gabe as we ran down the stairs into the burning rig from hell. The storm was so loud I couldn't hear anything. Then I heard a hammering sound. I stopped and looked at Gabe. "Do you hear that?"

"Yes, it's coming from over there." We ran to a closed door. My gloved hand hovered over the knob briefly before I pulled it open. Both of us stood back behind the door as I jerked it open. There were about twelve men there.

"Let's get the hell out of here!" I shouted. "Follow Gabe." I would stay in the back in case someone fell. I saw a woman stumble. *What the hell is a woman doing here?* I saw a man turn to see if she was still behind him. I walked up to her and picked her up. She felt perfect in my arms, and I had the strangest feeling.

"Please put me down. I assure you I can walk."

"The smoke is getting thick. We need to hurry before this entire platform explodes. I ran up the steps three at a time. Gabe had already started loading the men into the cage. I walked over and put the woman inside it.

"Why is a woman out here in the middle of the fucking ocean?" Gabe shouted.

"I'm the fucking inspector." I heard Gabe chuckle at the same time I did.

The cage swung out over the rough waves. As the cage dangled out to sea, a massive wave slapped against it. I held my breath and kept my fingers crossed that the door stayed closed. I saw the woman holding the latch so it couldn't open. It took four trips before we were all on the ship. I threw some sweats and a tee shirt at Hutch. "Can you give these to the woman? I'm sure she's freezing."

"Yeah, I'll show her where the shower is."

4

GILLY

My teeth were chattering when someone handed me a towel, sweats, and a man's tee shirt. "Thank you."

"My name is Hutch Campbell. Follow me. I'll show you where the shower is."

I looked at him. "You remind me of someone."

"I have one of those faces," he said, smiling.

"No, it's your eyes. I'll remember. I have a memory like an elephant." I held onto the rails in the long hallway as we walked. The sea was rough. I had to hold on to the hand bars to keep myself from falling. The ship was huge, but it still rocked. I knew the guy was watching my body as we walked. That was the problem with having so many curves. Men thought they had the right to look. "This storm came out of nowhere. I'm surprised you were able to find us."

"We have excellent equipment for that. It looks like you might have an injury on the back of your leg." Okay, maybe he wasn't looking at my body. He was still talking.

"We do a lot of rescues on rigs. The oil companies make sure we have the best equipment. They don't want bad publicity. Here you go. The hot water will last ten minutes per shower. When you finish, we'll throw your clothes in the washer, so you can have your own clothes to wear. My brother's clothes will swallow you up. There is shampoo in there, also. I advise you to use that first before the hot water runs out.

"Thank you." I looked around and didn't waste time getting out of my clothes. I took my underclothes into the shower with me to wash them. I'll hang them to dry when I'm assigned a room. I was not letting anyone wash my underwear. I'll stuff them in my bag for now.

I hurried through washing my hair then I washed all the salt water off my body. When the water turned cold, I turned it off and dried myself on a large towel. The man was right. His brother's clothes did swallow me. *I'll hang on to them, so they don't fall.* When I opened the door, someone stood there waiting for me.

"I'll show you to your room. One of the guys told us you were all in that room for two days. I'm sure you're hungry and tired. My name is Gabe. Hutch said you might have an injury to your leg. If you need someone to look at it, one of our buddies is a doctor. We'll have him check it out."

"It's nice to meet you, Gabe. I think my leg is fine, but I'll get it checked out. Thank you for asking. Some of the guys got angry because I made them stay in that room for two days. I knew they would die if I didn't make them stay there.

"We were lucky there was a toilet connected to the room. They would have been swept out to sea if they had left the room. We needed to keep the fire under control. The fire would have spread so fast if they had started opening doors. Oil was everywhere. It would have engulfed that rig before they knew what was happening. No one would have made it out of there alive.

"We lost one man when he panicked and ran to the top, trying to stay away from the fire. Now someone will have to tell his family. I've had to do that before, and it's not something I want to do again." We entered a cafeteria. Most of the crew was there eating.

"I'm sorry someone died. Take a seat, and I'll fix you a plate."

I was sitting in the cafeteria corner when someone sat down across from me. I looked up, then I smiled.

"Hello, Gilly."

I turned my head, and there he was, the man I'd thought of him so many times. That one kiss, I'll never forget it. "Grayson, I've often wondered what happened to my wrong date," *I wouldn't tell him how sometimes I would think of him for days at a time.*

"I joined the Navy Seals. How have you been?"

"Good, I work for the big oil companies. But thinking about handing in my notice. I often wondered how your real date went."

I laughed as I told her about my date with Gilda. We both laughed.

"We shouldn't laugh."

"What about your date?"

"He was sitting on my steps when I returned to my place. He was a nice guy. We went to dinner. It was nice."

"My dad had a heart attack that night."

"I'm sorry."

"Yeah, I moved home and never went back. Dad lived for two months after that. I told him about you. He said I should go back and see if you want to go to dinner with me. But when I did, you had already moved."

"Yeah, I was hired to inspect oil rigs on land and sea. And here I am still working for them."

"Can I take you out to dinner when we get back?"

"I would have liked nothing more, but I'm seeing somene right now."

"Well then, I'll keep asking, until you say yes."

"He wants to get married, but I need to make sure it's for real. I never thought I would see you again." The guy who gave me the clothes sat down next to Gray.

"Gilly, this is my brother, Hutch."

"No wonder I thought I knew you. Your eyes are the same as my wrong date."

"Gilly, was your wrong blind date?" Hutch asked, staring at me.

"Yes, small world, right?"

"Yeah, small world."

I saw the sadness in his brother's eyes and wondered about it. I stood up. "If you two will excuse me, I need to sleep for a while."

"I'll show you the way," Grayson said, standing up.

"Thank you, Hutch has already shown me." I held onto my borrowed sweats. "Hey, these must belong to you. Thanks for the loan of them."

"You're welcome."

God, why did I feel like I wanted to cry? I wiped my hand across my face, and there were tears there. *What is the matter with me? Is it because I always thought Gray Campbell was my one true love?*

But that was when you were younger. You are thirty-two now, and you know better. That's how stupid I was back then. True love, what an idiot I was at twenty-four.

He never came back to see me because his dad had a heart attack. It had nothing to do with that wild, hot kiss he gave me. *I can't think about him anymore. I've had that talk with myself before.*

I'm seeing someone right now. I can't remember one special kiss out of all the kisses I've had from Gerald. What is wrong with me? I never forgot the kiss Grayson Campbell gave me eight years ago. (You're thirty-two years old, Gilly; stop thinking about Grayson.)

What's crazy is I never became serious with another man because I compared all of their kisses to that one—*that one frigging kiss*. I probably imagined how it was anyway. What am I thinking I am seeing another man. I'm becoming serious about him. *Remember that, Gillian. You are serious about Gerald.*

I went to sleep, and I dreamed about Grayson Campbell. And in my dreams, we did a lot more than kiss.

5

GRAY

I couldn't believe my eyes when I saw Gilly eating at the table. I rubbed my eyes, and sure enough, there she was—all that beautiful brunette hair and those dark emerald eyes. I've dreamed of her for years. She still looked like she did back then, laughing at us getting our dates mixed up. She was the woman I picked up and put in the cage. No wonder I felt that feeling when I picked her up. It was the same feeling I had that one time I kissed her.

She's seeing someone. Stop it. For crying out loud, you're acting like an idiot. But she's not married. Stay away from her, Gray! You're acting like a man who hadn't had sex in a year when it was two weeks ago. Stop already!

I was in the cafeteria when she walked in for breakfast. I smiled as I watched her pick out what she wanted. She looked around and spotted me. I waved her over. She chewed her bottom lip. It was that lip that made me kiss her the first time. I knew she was trying to decide whether to sit with me, and I knew why. She wanted me as much as I wanted her. She finally made up her mind and walked toward me.

"I wasn't sure you would join me for breakfast."

"I wasn't sure if I would either." She took a bite of her scrambled eggs. "I want to be honest with you. I dreamed of you last night, and it wasn't about that kiss. It was much more than that. I think you're too tempting for me to be around."

I smiled. "How do you know I'm not married? Don't you think we can be friends? Men and women can be friends without having sex."

"Do you really think that? I have a lot of male friends, but I don't dream about them. Are you married?"

"No, I'm not. Of course, we can be friends."

"Okay, we will be friends."

She put her hand out, and I took it in mine. That same feeling when we met for the first time went through me. I wondered what I was getting myself into. *This will work. We can be friends until it doesn't work.*

"So, tell me what you've been doing besides becoming serious about the guy you are seeing. And having to be rescued from oil rigs out in the ocean," I said, staring at her lips as she chewed her plump bottom lip.

"If we are going to be friends, you must stop staring at my lips."

"Sorry, but you have to leave that plump bottom lip alone. It's getting me hot."

I watched as her eyes got all dreamy looking, and I knew without a doubt that we would be having hot sex before the day ended.

"You have to stop saying stuff like that. Friends don't talk about how hot they are for each other... I mean, for me... Never mind. I'm going to eat my breakfast, and then I'm going up on the top deck. I want to see if the storm is still tearing into the ocean."

"I'll go with you. I've been there this morning, so I know it's still there. It's supposed to calm down today. So, what have you been up to lately?"

"Working, I'm a workaholic. That's why my boss doesn't want me to quit."

"Tell me about your boyfriend who wants to get married. Is he afraid he'll lose you if he doesn't hurry and put a ring on your finger?"

"He knows he won't lose me. Putting your name on a piece of paper doesn't change anything."

"That's not a very romantic way to think about your wedding. Don't you want the works?"

"Not really. To me, you don't have to get married to stay with someone. If you love them, you'll stay with them. If you stop loving them, you'll go your separate ways, whether you are married or not."

"Do you live with your boyfriend?"

"No, we live in our own separate homes."

"I take it you aren't a romantic."

"No, I'm not. My mom was married three times and was miserable with all of them. The reason was she loved my father to distraction. She couldn't get over him. When I was three, my father was killed overseas. He was a Marine. My sister Lucy is two years older than me and married to her third husband. That's why I don't think a piece of paper can change anything. If you love someone, you will be with them until they leave, or you do."

"You're breaking my heart. You don't know anything about true love. It's heart-wrenching. You feel you are the luckiest person in the world to have that person's love. You are treasured by someone who loves you more than anything on earth."

"So, I take it you've felt this way before. Where is she? You must not love her if you want hot, sweaty sex with me."

"I never said sweaty."

I looked at her, and I knew she wanted me. It was in her eyes. "No, I've never felt that way. My father told me how he felt about my mom. But you were right about the hot, sweaty sex. I could make love to you all day and night and never get enough. What do you say? Do we go to my room or up on deck?"

Gilly gazed into my eyes as if she struggled to decide which choice she would pick. In a breathy voice, she whispered. "Up on deck."

I chuckled and stood up. I held out my hand, and she ignored it.

We put our trays away and walked up on deck. The wind was blowing hard, and the waves were huge. I loved it, and by the look on Gilly's face, she loved it too. "Shall we go to the front?"

"Yes," she laughed, taking my hand, "this is amazing!"

I wrapped my arm around her as we made our way to the front of the ship.

"Watch those waves?" we heard over the speaker. I turned my head and gave Hutch a thumbs-up.

"This is crazy. I love it. Why do you think that is?"

"I'm the same way. Do you do anything extreme?"

"Yes, I love to surf in the highest waves possible. I go to Australia every year to surf. It drives Gerald crazy."

"Is that your boyfriend?"

"Yes, Gerald Spencer."

"Gerald Spencer; is he your boss?"

"Yes, he's been my boss for eight years. We started dating a year ago."

"You're going to get wet!" I shouted as a huge wave hit us.

Our feet went so high in the air that it was a good thing we were holding on to the railing. "We need to get back. It's too rough," Gilly looked at me and smiled. Then another look came over her, and I was hard in the blink of an eye. I took her hand, and we ran back inside. I walked down the hall and stopped at my door. "Are you sure?"

"No, but I need to have hot, sweaty sex with you. I ache to my core with wanting you. I want you deep inside me."

I opened my door and pulled her tee shirt over her head. Then I unbuttoned her wet pants and pulled them down. I heard her moan as I peeled her panties off. I was starting to hurt. My jeans were too tight. My hot breath chuckled against her lips. My fingers entered her I thought she would climb on top of me. She was so hot.

I picked her up and laid her on the bed. I continued to please her. I touched her soft spot. I raised myself and reached to taste her breast, which fit my large hands perfectly. I let my tongue trace the nipple. Then I kissed her. I kissed her like I had wanted to kiss her for eight years. After eight years of wanting her, I would take my time. No one would be rushing me. My hand slipped between her thighs and inside her wetness again.

"More, give me more," Gilly cried.

My fingers worked faster. Gilly's breathing was fast. I knew when she was ready to come, screaming her orgasm into my neck. Over and over, she orgasmed then I slipped myself inside her. I went slow at first until she got over her orgasms.

She was almost crying as she orgasmed again, and then I let myself orgasm. We both lay there breathing hard. I braced myself on my elbows, kissing her face. Until she noticed I was still as hard as ever, she started moving her body, driving mine crazy.

I looked at her and smiled. "Are you sure you want it again?"

"Yes, I'm sure."

I shouted out my orgasm into her neck. I collapsed onto the bed next to her.

"The next time won't be as fast. My body wasn't in control. I'll be in control next time," I said, pulling Gilly close and kissing her neck.

"Next time, are you kidding me? I'm still having orgasms from the first time. I've never done that before."

"You've never done what before?"

"I've never had so many orgasms. It was mind-blowing."

I pushed against Gilly so she could feel how ready I was for her. She reached down, her hand circled me, and then she climbed on me. She straddled my lap and slid down. She started moving fast. I grabbed her hips and helped her. I had to force myself not to shout her name for every person on the ship to hear. I had never felt this way, and I'd had plenty of sex. We lay still for a few minutes, and then she cuddled into my side.

"That was the best sex I've ever had," she whispered.

"You ain't seen nothing yet," I chuckled. Both of us slept. When I woke up, an hour passed, and Gilly had gone. I got up and showered.

6

GILLY

I couldn't believe I had sex like that with someone who wasn't my boyfriend. I didn't even know him. Meeting him once years ago didn't mean diddly squat. I didn't know this man, and I didn't know if I could face him again. His face was buried in my crotch, for crying out loud, and I screamed for more. Just, thinking about him was making me want him again.

Just because you had the best sex you ever had in your entire thirty-one years on earth does not mean anything. Stop it right now. You cannot have him. You are involved with a kind, loving man. Gerald loves you.

I could not stay inside my room for the rest of my time here. I was no better than my mother. At least I knew what she meant when she and Lucy discussed great sex. Lucy only said that about her first husband. *I can't let this happen again. I'll have to tell Gerald. Maybe I won't have to say anything.* I wondered how long I would be on this ship.

Someone knocked, and I reluctantly opened my door. It was another man. I think his name was Gabe. "I came to tell you Gerald Spencer phoned the ship. He's sending a helicopter for you. The weather is clearing up. We aren't that far from the port, but he wants to ensure you are alright."

"Thank you. Do you know when he'll be here?"

"In twenty minutes. You can meet him up top."

"Thank you. I'll be right there."

I looked around. I had to put the sweats and sweatshirt back on. My clothes were still soaked, so I folded them and left them in the bathroom. *Will I see Gray before I go?* I realized I was silently crying and wiped my face with his sweatshirt.

Stop it! You're acting like an idiot. This was a one-time fling. It was built up over the years because of that one kiss eight years ago. I didn't want to leave. I looked around and knew I wanted to stay, but I couldn't. I had responsibilities I had to take care of. *If Gray and I are meant to be together, we'll find each other again.* I stood straight and opened my door, and walked out. Gray stood there. He pushed me back inside and took my face in his hands.

"Stay with me. We belong together. You know that."

"I don't know that. We have good chemistry and great sex, the greatest sex. That's what we have. It's lust. I've never felt like this, and I'm scared and confused. We knew eight years ago it would be like this. I can't hurt him because I lust for you. He loves me—" Gray's lips crushed mine.

His hands were in my hair, and he plundered my mouth. I didn't want him to stop. I knew I had to push him away. "I have to go. Goodbye, Gray." He didn't say a word. He didn't even turn around. I walked up top, and the helicopter was landing.

Gerald jumped out and ran to me. He pulled me into his arms. "God, Gilly, I was so scared. I'm so thankful that you are safe." He kissed me, and a tear slipped from my eyes.

"Let's go, okay? I want to get into some of my own clothes."

"Why are you wearing these? What happened to your clothes?"

"I got caught in the storm this morning." He put his arm around me and guided me to the copter. After I was settled in my seat, I looked around. I saw Gray standing next to his brother. My hand touched the window, and then I let it fall. *So, this is another chapter in my life with Grayson Campbell.*

"Are you okay, honey?"

"Yes, I'm just tired. It'll be nice to get back to my place."

"Why don't you come to my place? I want to make sure you are alright. I don't like you being alone. When I heard about the fire, I was so fucking scared. I couldn't get to you. Thank goodness I was able to call Seals Security."

I was shaking my head. I didn't want to go home with Gerald. "I want to go to my place. Right now, I only want to soak in a tub, climb into bed, and sleep. Is that alright? Tomorrow we'll spend the day together."

"If you're sure, then that's what we will do. Are you okay? Nothing happened when you were on the rig, did it?"

"Well, that man died, so of course, that upset me. Has someone talked to his family?"

"Yes, Sherry talked to them."

"Sherry, was that a good idea? She doesn't have an ounce of compassion in her body."

"I was too upset with you being stuck on the burning rig. I didn't even realize she was the one going until Joe reminded me she went to talk to the family. I guess she did okay. I haven't heard any complaints."

He put his arm around me. At first, I stiffened, but then I relaxed. This was my friend, my boyfriend. I lay my head on his shoulder.

"I quit. I don't want to work with your company any longer." I didn't want to talk to Gerald right now. All I wanted to think about was Gray. I tried to remember every word spoken between Gray and me. You would think I was in love with the man.

"You're just tired. Once we get you home, you'll feel better. Then we can talk about your job. Why don't we get married this month, and then we'll start our family, and you can stay home with our babies."

I stared at him like he had two heads. *What the hell is he talking about? I'm not going to do any of that.* "Gerald, you know that's not me. I'm not staying home when I'm ready to have a child. I would go crazy not working, and we are not getting married this month."

"But you just quit your job."

"I'm going to get a different one. I'm not going to worry about it right now. I will visit my mom and sister for a while before deciding what to do. I know I need a break from all of this." I raised my head and saw the city. I let out a sigh. *This will be hard, but I can't be with a man when I want another one. I'll tell him tomorrow.*

"Look, dear, we are almost home."

"I've never been so happy to see dry land," I said, and Gerald tightened his arm around me and kissed me on the mouth. It was so unlike him to kiss me in public. I was surprised at first and started to pull away. Then I made myself stop. I only felt sadness. I didn't want to hurt Gerald. *Maybe I will feel differently in a few weeks. I'll wait and see.*

What are you thinking? There is nothing to wait and see. You had sex with another man—the best sex in your life. Your heart is hurting because you left him behind. You have to tell Gerald. You cannot be with someone while wanting someone else. I can't be with Gerald when I know I don't love him. The car drove me home, and I sighed with relief.

"Why don't I come in with you?"

I looked at him and felt sad, knowing I would be hurting him. "All I want is to take a long hot bath and sleep. I'll see you tomorrow." I opened the car door and gave Gerald a quick kiss goodbye. I walked into my condo. It felt like I had been gone forever. I felt like I'd changed completely. I've always been so careful in my life because I didn't want to be like my mom or sister, but I had sex with another man while being with someone else.

I'm no better than them. I know Lucy was trying to get Adam, her first husband and the only man she has ever loved, to do something. She thought if she made him jealous, he would demand she marry him again.

I always wondered how she could have sex with someone else, knowing she would only ever love one man. Now I know you must have a lot of willpower over your body, and I had none over mine when I was near Gray. I often wondered if Lucy had sex with Adam while married to the other guys.

I started my bath and stripped out of Gray's clothes. I inhaled them as I held them to my face. *I'm pathetic; what is wrong with me?* I climbed into the tub and sank beneath the water. When I raised my head out of the water, I couldn't tell where the water had ended, and the tears began. I had to think. I needed to plan. I had already quit my job.

I didn't have to worry about running out of money; I had enough saved to last years. But I knew I would find another job. *Where do I want to live?* I remember my friend from college talking about her hometown in Oregon. To me, it sounded like the best place to live. What was the name of that town? I think it was Cedar Falls. As soon as I got out of the bath, I googled Cedar Falls. I fell in love with the small town just by looking at it.

It was time I began a new life. I don't want to work seven days a week. I want to enjoy my life and work three days a week. That would be perfect. *What business can I do if I only want to work three days a week?* Well, I didn't have to figure out everything right now.

I could take my time. *I will talk to Gerald tomorrow.* That would be the hardest thing I've ever done in my life. Then I would put my condo up for sale. It would be hard to break up with him because he was my friend, and I loved him, but not as he loved me.

I decided to call my mom and see what she was doing. *Maybe I'll visit her before I move.* I had almost hung up when she answered the phone. She was out of breath.

"Hello."

"Hi, Mom. What are you doing?"

"I just got home. I've been worried about you. Lucy and I have both been hunting for you. Where have you been?"

"I was on a rig in the ocean, and it caught fire. There was this massive storm, and one man wouldn't listen when I told him to stay in the room, and he died. I just got home. I quit my job."

"It's about time. It was sucking all the youth out of you. Now, did you break up with Gerald?"

"No, but I will tell him I don't want to keep seeing him tomorrow. It's going to be hard because he's my friend." I started crying. I must have shocked my mom because she was speechless. Then when she opened her mouth, I wished she wouldn't have.

"What have you done?"

"Do you remember my wrong date?"

"How could I forget the way you explained that kiss?"

"He rescued me from the rig."

"Don't say another word. I'm making this a three-way call."

"Lucy, Gilly is going to tell us about her wrong date. Remember, his name was Gray. Go ahead. Gilly, start from the beginning."

"I was stuck on a burning rig in the ocean for a few days. One man wouldn't listen to me to stay in one room, and the poor man died a horrible death. We were rescued from the burning rig in this massive storm by some former Navy Seals on this huge ship. One of those men was my wrong date. He's more handsome than I remembered. It's been eight years. There is not one ounce of fat on him, and believe me, I know because I had sex with him."

I sniffed so they knew I was crying. "It was so amazing; I've never had so many orgasms. I swear, just thinking of it makes me want more. He wanted me to stay with him when Gerald came to get me with his helicopter. I went with Gerald..." *I couldn't believe I was discussing having hot sex with my mom and sister. I was as bad as the both of them.*

I was crying and blowing my nose. I waited for them to speak, and finally, Lucy said something, "Are you frigging crazy? Why would you go with Gerald? You found the man who is your true love from eight years ago and blew it.

I remember thinking how lucky you were when you told us that story, about that kiss. I would give anything to find a connection like that. Plus, all those orgasms. Find him and get back on that ship. Please do whatever you must, but don't blow it again. What are you going to do about Gerald?"

"I'm going to break up with him tomorrow. I have already quit my job."

"After you break up with him, come home for a few days.

Mom and I never get to see you anymore. We miss you, Gilly."

"I miss you too. I'll be there the day after tomorrow. Mom, I'll stay with you. Will that be okay?"

"Of course, it will, sweetheart. I can't wait to see you. I'll air your room out. Drive careful, sweetie. We love you."

"I will. I love you guys too."

Okay, I blew that conversation all to hell. I was not supposed to tell Mom and Lucy about Gray. When you see them, keep your lips sealed for crying out loud. I pretended to zip my lips. *I will not let them make me talk. Besides, I've already told them everything there was to tell.*

7

GRAY

I missed her, damn it. I wasn't going to miss her. I asked her to stay. Okay, that would have been odd with her boyfriend waiting with a helicopter. I have never felt like this. When I saw her sitting at that table, my heart soared. It wasn't just the sex. I admit that was amazing. It was everything. I felt like we connected on so many levels. *When we get back to port, I'll see her, and we'll talk and see where it goes from here. I can wait two weeks. She isn't going anywhere, plus I know where she works.*

"Gray, are you going to eat?"

"Yes," I said. The sun was shining bright as I opened the door. As soon as I walked into the mess hall, I laughed. There was a cake with my name on it. I hadn't been keeping count of the days, but leave it to Hutch to remember my birthday. We had dinner and then cake. Hutch handed me an envelope with something in it. I opened it, and there were photos of Gilly and me standing up top in the storm, laughing at each other. In some, we were eating. She wore my clothes in most of them. I loved this gift. "I don't know how you did this, but I'm glad you did. Thank you."

Jackson handed me a package. I looked in it, and Gilly's clothes were inside, folded up and laundered. "Your excuse for going to see her."

"This is perfect. Thanks, Jackson. Leave it to you to always think about how to stay in touch with a woman."

"Only some women. My experience is, if they're clingers, stay away from them."

"Yes, we know you love them and leave them."

"Some I keep around longer than others. All of you are the same way as I am. Don't try saying that's not true."

Hutch looked around at all of us. "While everyone is here, I want to talk to you about something. I got a call from Ryker. He's started up a security team of Seals. It's called Seals Security. The main offices will be from our hometown, Cedar Falls. Who wants to go into partnership with him?"

"I'm in," I said right away. They all cheered. Everyone was tired of working for the oil companies.

"What a relief; I was going to quit after this run," Gabe said. "Now, I won't have to."

"Okay, we have two months to finish what we're doing. I'll let our oil bosses know this is the last run. Then we will be on dry land working," Hutch said, smiling. "I thought most of you would want to join. I'm glad it's our team. I'll see if I can contact some of the others. We're equal partners. We all love Mace, but he's taken the wrong path to hell. Until he stops his drinking and whatever else he's doing, he can't join until he straightens up. Not that he would want to join. I'm sure he would throw a fist in my face if he saw me.

"I haven't seen Mace in a few years," Gabe said. "I doubt he would want to join. He stays in the bars most of the time. His mom is so worried about him. It's been five years since the accident, and I don't think he's had one sober day. He wrecked his bike. I think he ran off the cliff because he wanted to. I went to visit him when he was in the hospital. He doesn't look like the same guy. He told me he wanted to die. That was two years ago."

I shook my head. I've known Mace since we were in kindergarten. We joined the service together. "Yeah, I saw him the last time I was in Cedar Falls. He was at the Wild Cat bar, and he was in a fight with three guys. He walloped all of them. I think he's bigger than he used to be. I tried to get him to let me drive him home, but he declined. Maybe he stopped trying to kill himself. I hope so."

I went to Gilly's work carrying her clothes in the same package that Jackson gave me. I looked around the area, and a blonde was at the front desk. "How can I help you."

"I'm looking for Gillian Marshall."

"Gilly no longer works here."

I ran my hand threw my unruly curls. I usually have them so short I don't notice the curls. But I decided to let my hair grow out. "I'm from the ship that rescued her and those men. I have her clothes that were soaked. They have been laundered, and I wanted to return them to her. Can you tell me where she lives?"

The woman looked around to see if anyone could hear her. "Gilly sold her condo and moved away. We were all in shock. We thought for sure her and the boss would get married, but she broke up with him," she whispered.

My blood started pumping fast. *Gilly broke up with him.* "Do you have her phone number?"

"No, I couldn't give it to you even if I did."

"Can you tell me where she lived? Maybe I can get a number from a neighbor."

"I don't have that information. H.R. has all that info. I'm sorry I couldn't be more helpful."

"That's okay. I'll google her." I almost skipped back to the ship.

Hutch looked at me when I got back. He noticed I still carried her clothes. "You didn't find her?"

"She broke up with her boyfriend and sold her house. She moved away. I couldn't find out where she had moved to. But I will find her. I lost her once for eight years, and we found each other."

****

"That sounds like a romance book. Maybe you should become a writer. You know Mom loves reading those romance novels."

"Oh my God, my brother has turned into a comic. When is your first show? I'll be sure and miss it."

Both of us laughed. But Hutch knew how serious I was. I've talked about Gilly for eight years, and after making love to her, I knew I would never forget her. She belongs to me. She knows it, and I know I will find her. I didn't care how long it took me. I figured it shouldn't take me too long.

Okay, maybe it would take longer than I thought. I've been home for a month, and it's been three months since I last saw Gilly. First, we had so many jobs lined up that I couldn't sit still long enough to hunt for her. And now I was sent out of the country to bring home a teenage girl who ran off with some of her older friends who were groupies to a hard rock band.

If she were lucky, her parents wouldn't kill her. They have had everyone in the United States hunting for her. They thought she was kidnapped or murdered. Sometimes seventeen-year-olds thought they were old enough to do what they wanted. I think when I turned sixteen was when I thought I knew everything.

I was in England walking to the hotel when I spotted her

crying across the street from where she was staying. I recognized the girl as Zoe Loftin. "Why are you crying?"

"I don't talk to strangers."

"Are you kidding me? You ran off with a bunch of groupies following a hard rock band, and you don't talk to strangers."

"Who are you?"

"I'm Gray Campbell from Seal's Security. I've come to take you home."

"I wanted my mom to come and get me."

"No, you're way better off having me. Your parents are mad enough to chew nails. They had the entire country hunting for you. They thought you were dead."

"Then they should be jumping for joy because I'm alive."

"It doesn't work that way. First, when you called, they were so relieved you were alive. Then, when you told them you ran off without a word to anyone, they were hurt that you would be so immature that you would do something like that. I mean, seventeen; none of the seventeen-year-olds I know would ever do this to their parents." It didn't hurt to lie a bit. I didn't know what a seventeen-year-old would or would not do.

"Am I going to be lectured the entire ride home?"

"No. Where are your things?"

"The hotel has them. They won't return them because I owe them for two nights."

"Follow me."

I walked across the street, and the girl followed behind me. When I got to the registration desk, the man pointed his finger at her, "Get out unless you can pay for your stay."

"Wow, you talk like that to your patrons in front of other guests. I'll have to call my friend who owns this hotel and let him know what's going on," I said, frowning. "I won't be staying here. Felix is your name? I'll be sure and tell him."

"She owes for two nights. It's our policy to remove any guest who hasn't paid their bill."

"I'll pay her bill." I turned around and looked at her, "Is there something you need to get from your room?"

"Her belongings are in the basement closet. That's where we take things left behind."

"They weren't left behind. You took her belongings from her room." We got her belongings and headed back to the airport. The plane didn't leave until midnight, so we had dinner at the airport. Zoe fell asleep, and I woke her up when it was time for us to go.

We were getting ready to land when she started to cry again. "Look, let me give you some advice. From this moment on, how you choose to live your life is how your life will turn out. If you want a good life, one you can tell your kids about, then remember that everything you do has a consequence. Before you do something, think to yourself and say, 'Do I want to do this?' You control everything, who your friends are and who you want to keep as your friends. It's all in your hands."

"I know. I was so stupid. I'm ashamed to see my parents and my little sisters. They will think it's okay to do anything they want because of what I did. I'll talk to them and tell them how stupid I was. Thank you for picking me up."

"You're welcome."

8

GILLY

I ended up staying with my mom for six months. I almost let my mom talk me into buying a home there. My mother was a realtor broker. She was a very popular realtor in Santa Barbara, California. It was nice visiting with her and Lucy. They were so much alike. Lucy wasn't happy with her third husband.

She wanted a divorce, but because she was on her third husband and thirty-three, she decided to put up with him for a few more years until the baby was older. Lucy had three kids, one with her first husband, one with her second, and one with her third. She was beautiful. Lucy was what men called a knockout. Plus, she had such a kind heart. She couldn't get over Adam. I believe her first husband was her soul mate. But he always had motorcycle gangs hanging out with him.

I caught up with my old friends. Most of them were married with kids. One of my friends said I was so afraid of turning into my mom and sister I was scared to marry anyone. I wondered if that was true. Who knows? I knew I couldn't be with anyone while Grayson Campbell was still on my mind. I still have wet dreams about Gray. Sometimes, I don't want to get out of bed. All I had to do was remember everything he did to me.

I was lying on the beach when someone sat down beside me. "Hey, beautiful, what are you doing lying in all this sun?"

Fuck, I was hoping to stay away from this jerk. "Hello, Ron. What brings you to the beach?"

"Someone told me you were in town, so I knew the sun goddess would be on the beach somewhere. I also heard you broke up with your fiancé. Now, how about dinner and a fuck with me tonight?"

"I see you haven't changed at all. Still as vile as you always were. I am not going anywhere with you, so please get the fuck away from me."

"Gilly, Gilly, Gilly. You know you have always belonged to me. I was your first, and I will be your last. That's something you should remember."

"You don't scare me anymore, Ron. I'm all grown up now. I'm not a scared teenager who you raped."

"There was no rape, and you know it. You wanted me then, and you want me now. I'm not blind; I can see all the messages you silently send me. We will go to my house if you don't want to go out. Gilly, never forget I have ways of making you do things. I never did anything that you didn't deserve. You treat me right, and you get treated right. You belong to me."

"Go fuck yourself." The next thing I knew, he was lying on top of me. To the people around us, he looked like a lover kissing me. He pushed his hand down my bathing suit and pushed his fingers into me. He was strong. I couldn't move him. I tried crying for help, and he put his mouth over mine. He ground his teeth into my lips until I tasted blood. I almost let him scare me, like in high school. I pushed with all my might until he jumped up.

"You stay the fuck away from me, or I will kill you."

"How much do you love those nieces of yours? I wonder if Lucy would miss one of them if I took one."

"You think you can control me. You don't scare me anymore. You come around anyone I love, and you are dead."

"I'll pick you up at six. Be there and be ready for me. I want you to wear that dress you were wearing Monday. And, Gilly, no panties." I watched him walk away. I was shaking inside. I was so scared. Ron controlled my life all through my junior year. He would beat me and threaten my family. I was a terrified teenager until he went away to college, and I never saw him after that. Then I left for college. I never came home. I was so scared of running into him. Finally, I told my mother what had happened, and we cried together.

Mom talked to the police, and they wanted me to tell them everything he had done to me. I didn't want the other kids to know what happened. The police said they would keep an eye on him. Even when I went away to school that first year, I was frightened, he would show up. I felt sorry for the poor girl who took my place. *I will not let him control my life.*

I stopped by Mom's office and told her everything. "Mom, he scares me. I'm leaving today. He said he would take one of Lucy's kids away and kill them. He looks like he is more warped in his head than he was. He was raping me on the beach. Mom, he held me down, and I couldn't move. It was as if I was a teenager again. I was so scared. I started crying. I have to leave. I don't want to go home alone and pack my things."

"I'll go with you, sweetheart, don't worry, that bastard

will not get away with this. I'm going to call John. He was the police officer I talked to about Ron when you were young. I've kept my eyes on him. I believe he hit all his girlfriends. I will call Lucy and tell her, she will keep an eye on the girls. I also told Lucy about Ron because he started hanging around with Adam."

When six o'clock came around, John answered the door at my mom's house. My first brother-in-law was there. He threw Ron against the wall. "Don't you ever threaten to take my daughters, you fucking bastard? I'll kill your fucking ass right now. You stay away from my family."

"What is wrong with you? I only had a little fun with Gilly. All I did was ask her out for dinner and a fuck. Don't you ever push me around? You better watch your back."

I was hiding around the corner but saw Adam's fist land in Ron's face. "You get the fuck out of here and don't come back. I'll take you to the dunes if I hear anything else about you. And you know what happens to the people there."

"Fuck all of you." He turned and walked away.

Adam turned and looked at me. "I'm sorry about what happened to you. We'll do some investigating and check other women he's dated."

"Who's we?"

"My biker friends and me."

"Adam, I don't want you getting into trouble with the law."

"Hey, Bean, don't worry about me. I can take care of myself and mine. You take care of yourself."

"I'll be careful."

"Are you back for good?"

"No, I'm leaving tomorrow." He smiled and left. I watched his Harley until it was out of sight. I used to have the biggest crush on him. I mean, who wouldn't? He's so hot.

But he's my ex-brother-in-law. I turned and looked at mom and John. They were watching me.

"It would be best if you didn't go anywhere alone. I've been watching him. He's had a couple of reports of abuse, but no one has pressed charges."

"I'm leaving in the morning. Can you come by and make sure Ron stays away from my mom?"

"Yes, I will. I need to get going. You, ladies, take care of yourself."

"Thank you, John. I'll walk out with you."

I turned, and Lucy was wiping her eyes. "Do you still love him?"

"More than anything in the world, I will always love him. But I had to get out of that life. Bikers were always at our house. I had a baby. I asked him to decide what he wanted to do. He didn't see anything wrong. He watched me leave. He broke his hand, slugging the wall. When I got to work, he was in one of the cubicles. I was shocked to see him at the hospital. I didn't wait on him; I called another nurse to take care of his hand."

"He's still so frigging hot. I used to have a crush on him."

"I know. Everyone had a crush on Adam Wilson. You be careful and watch for Ron. He's going to be angry because Adam busted his nose."

"Do you think he'll come after me when I move away?"

"Who knows what that freak will do? Adam will kill him if he even drives past my house. I wish you could live here with us. Don't you enjoy being with your family?"

"I love being here. But I have always been on my own. Even when I lived at home, you and mom were always off somewhere together. I've already found a building for my coffee shop. It was already a coffee shop, so I bought everything. You should come and stay a while and teach me to make those delicious donuts you make."

"You're an engineer, Gilly. You build things. Are you going to waste your career and open a coffee shop?"

"Yes."

"Well, then, I can't wait to come and visit you."

I walked over to her and hugged her. "I'm so glad we got to spend this time together."

"I love you, little sister."

"I love you too."

9
GRAY

"Gray, come back to bed."

I hate myself! I didn't want to go back in there. I fucking hate myself! The next thing I knew, Sharon stepped into the shower with me. Her arms went around me, and she took my cock in her hand. I didn't want to do this. I turned around, and my hands held her arms. "Sharon, I need to leave. I'm sorry, I don't have time for more. I'm already late. I'm meeting my brother in ten minutes."

"your buddies won't mind you being late."

"I will mind. This business is important to all of us."

"Come back for dinner." I was drying off and barely kept myself from making a face. I was drunk last night and let Sharon talk me into going to her place. I dated her a while back after my dad died. I already regretted coming here last night. I was so fucking stupid. What the hell was the matter with me?

I dressed and turned to Sharon. I hated doing this. I ran my fingers through my hair. "Look, Sharon. I didn't mean to lead you on. Last night shouldn't have happened. It's been a while since I've had sex. The reason for that is because I'm in love with someone, and if I ever have the time, I'm going after her."

"We can hang out and enjoy each other until you do that."

"No, I'm sorry, you don't understand. I don't want to be with anyone except Gilly.

"Gilly, what a crazy name. So I guess a quicky now and then is against the rules."

"For me, it is." I hurried and put my shoes on. I was so fucking angry at myself for allowing this to happen.

"I should have married you when I had a chance."

I couldn't remember giving her a chance. We dated a few times, and then I left. "Goodbye, Sharon."

"I'll see you around, Gray."

I got the hell out of there and walked back to my vehicle. When a pickup pulled up to my side, I shut my eyes. This is not what I wanted to happen. I wanted to forget about last night. Now Gabe and Jackson knew about it. I'm sure they saw me coming from Sharon's.

"Want a ride to your truck?"

I looked at them. "Not one word." I opened the back door and climbed inside. We drove the two miles to my vehicle. "Thanks. I'll see you at the meeting." I stopped and got myself a cup of coffee and an apple fritter. The Coffee Shop had been sold. I hoped whoever bought it would keep the donuts and great coffee.

The building was already packed when I walked inside our new building. The Seals purchased the property and built a building so we could each have an office. We had too many calls, and we all needed our own office. Plus, we were interviewing for a receptionist. We needed someone who knew how to work a computer.

When I walked inside, they all stared at me. Hutch didn't look too happy. I should have known Gabe and Jackson wouldn't keep their mouth shut. "I don't want to hear anything. I have a headache and feel like I'm going to vomit."

"Let's get started. We need to recruit new Seals. I'm going to put the word out. We have to escort three kids to their dad. Their mother has to spend time in prison. We can't tell the dad beforehand because she doesn't want him to feel pressured to help her. She'll have a letter for you to give him. Who wants to go?"

"I'll go, I said, reaching for the file. Jackson and Gabe agreed to go as well. We headed out the door, but Hutch called me back.

"What?"

"What happened last night?"

"I got drunk and went home with Sharon. Yes, I fucking regret it. I feel like shit. I don't want a lecture."

"She habitually takes guys to her home when she's at the bar. I don't want you to get caught up in her crap."

"Yes, Mother. Goodbye, Mother."

We caught the plane for Wyoming to pick up the kids. They were triplets, and they were four years old. They were the cutest little girls. Their mother, Hannah Lial, was a beauty. She wore blue jeans and cowboy boots. I asked her why she was going to prison. She said she slugged the judge when he put his hand under her dress and grabbed her butt. She is a waitress. I couldn't believe she had to go to prison over a slug in the face.

"Okay, listen to me. The girls' daddy doesn't know about them. I was hoping you could stay with them for a few days to ensure they are cared for." She was wiping tears from her face. "I have never been away from my babies overnight. I shouldn't have hit him, but he was so vile. We have to wear mini dresses at work. He ran his hand up my dress and squeezed my butt. What would you have done?"

"I would have knocked him on his ass. How long are they sending you to prison? This is fucking bullshit. You don't go to prison for slugging someone for groping you."

"Two years. My babies won't know me when I get out."

"Where is your family?"

"It's only me. My parents and my two brothers died in a car accident."

"Did you have a lawyer when you went to court?"

"They gave me a public defender, but he was the judge's nephew. Listen, I can only hope this man remembers me. I met him at a club in New York. I was there for my friend's wedding. We were together for three beautiful days. His name is Mace Cohen. He lives in Oregon. Please ask him if he will watch the girls until I get out. Then I want them back. I found his address. Here it is."

I looked at the others, and we all shook our heads. *Mace, I don't know how he's going to react.* He wasn't very stable when I last saw him. That's been a couple of years. He still lives in town, but would he take care of the girls? Only one way to find out. If he didn't, I know his mom would love them.

"We know Mace Cohen. He lives in our town. I know his mom will love these girls. So will Mace. He'll be in shock at first, but he loves kids."

"I know about Mace losing his family in that accident. We both lost our families the same way. But maybe he can find love again in his heart with the girls. The one with the pink bow is Abby, short for Abigail. The one with the purple bow is Ellie, and this one with the red bow is Annie. I've told them all about their daddy. It's best to keep the same colors on the girls that they now have on, so he can tell them apart. I can tell who is who, but no one else can. I don't want them to be afraid of him, so I've been preparing them. I don't want them to see me getting picked up by the police, so can I hug them one more time, and then you can take them to Mace."

She cried so hard when we took those babies out to our vehicle. I felt so bad for her. The first thing I was going to do was to sober Mace up. He's a lawyer. He can get her out of this mess. It was a fucking laugh. I wondered how old she was. I bet she was no more than thirty, if that old.

"Are you taking us to our daddy?" Annie asked.

"Yes, we are. Are you excited?"

"No, we aren't."

"I am Annie, and I want my mommy. I don't want our daddy."

"Don't start crying, Ellie. We don't want our daddy to think we are crybabies."

"I want my mommy," Abby said.

"How do you like riding in a plane?"

"I like it," Annie said. I noticed she was the talker out of the bunch. "What if our daddy doesn't want us?"

"He will want you. You also have a grandma who will love you. I'll call her, and she can meet us at Mace's house."

"Do we call him Daddy or Mace?" Annie asked.

"You can call him whatever you want to call him."

"I'm not scared. I just miss my mommy. She's the best mommy," Ellie said as big tears fell down her face. I reached over and picked her up, and hugged her. When I looked across the aisle at the others, they were crying too.

We were driving when I called Debra Cohen. "Well, I haven't heard from you in forever. What is going on?"

"We were hoping you could meet us over at Mace's

place. If he has anyone there, can you run them off? I have a surprise for both of you."

"Oh my, now you got me excited. How long do I have?

"You have thirty minutes." I knew that was no problem because Debra lived behind Mace's house. He sold his other home and bought this one. Then he built Debra a cottage behind his. His property was enormous. With her living there, it didn't get too rowdy. She would run everyone off.

"We'll see you in thirty minutes. Mace is fixing the fence. The wind was rough last night, and some of the fences fell over."

I pulled into his driveway, and we walked around back. I could see him working. He had his shirt off, and I noticed he had more tattoos. "Is that him?" Annie whispered. "He looks scary. Why is he so tall?"

I knew all the women said he looked hot, but I guess little girls would think he looked scary. I wish he would smile. "Mace, how are you doing?"

He put his equipment down and looked at the girls. He didn't say anything. The girls looked at him like they were in a staring contest.

Annie walked and stood right in front of him. "Are you our daddy?"

Debra put her hand over her mouth. Mace looked like he might run. But then he looked at me. "Tell me what is going on. I don't know who is pulling this shit, but I will kill them."

"You can't say shit. It's a nasty word. My mommy said people aren't allowed to talk like that around her girls." She looked at me, then ran to Debra, who gathered her in her arms. "Gray, will you take us back to our mommy? Please."

"Sweetheart, your mom is not allowed to see you right now. Let me talk to Mace, and he can sort everything out.

Here," I said, giving the letter to Mace. He walked away as he read the letter.

"Gray, what is going on? Debra said, looking at the three identical girls."

"These are your granddaughters. Abby has the pink bow, Ellie has the purple bow, and Annie has the red one. They've come to visit their grandma and daddy while their mommy goes to prison for slugging a judge in the face for putting his hand up her dress and groping her."

I watched as Ellie walked to Mace and took his hand. "Can I lay down, Daddy?"

We all thought Mace would cry hearing her call him daddy. He picked her up then he picked up Abby. Annie watched as he walked to her and picked her up. He held all three girls in his arms.

"You are strong. I won't be scared because my Daddy is strong. He won't let that mean judge take us away," Annie said, leaning her head on his shoulder.

"So you must be Annie, the one who does all the talking?"

"I was the first one to talk. I'm hungry, Daddy."

"I'm hungry too. Everyone, follow me. I'll make us lunch."

"I'll help," Debra said, wiping the tears from her face. "Three of you. My goodness. I have three granddaughters."

We brought the girls' suitcases in. The girls stood in the doorway looking in at Mace's house. Annie shook her head. "You have to clean the house. You are not supposed to have motorcycles in the house. We can help you. We always pick up our toys. I don't know what to pick up first."

"I'll tell you what. We'll eat at grandma's and stay there tonight. We will all camp out in some sleeping bags. I'll have this place cleaned up in no time. Grandma can take you to her house and start lunch. And these two will help me to move the motorcycle. I'll shower and be right there."

"Daddy, you won't leave us, will you?"

"I will never leave you. I'm your daddy, and daddies don't leave."

"That was easy—convincing you these girls were yours."

He didn't say anything. He walked into the kitchen and cried. We stayed where we were until he was ready to talk. Then he walked back to us, wiping his eyes.

"I didn't doubt it after I read Hannah's letter. I remember her like it was yesterday. She was at her friend's wedding. She looked so sad. I worried for her because she looked like she would start crying any minute, so I walked over to her, and you know what happened next. We were together for three days. Now I have three daughters." He shook his head. "They are beautiful."

"She wanted me to stay a couple of days to ensure you want them. I don't think I need to do that. Do you still get drunk every night? Are your biker friends still here every night?"

"I haven't gotten drunk in months. I don't hang with those guys anymore. I'm finished with all of that. I have something to live for now. Tell me why Hannah is in prison."

I told him everything Hannah told us. When I finished, he was ready to explode.

"Who is this joker? I'm calling in some favors the government owes me. Thank you for bringing my family to me. I'll send the check."

"This one is on us. But if you want to do something for us, you can work with the Seals Security and be our lawyer."

"I'll get back to you on that. It sounds interesting."

We said our goodbyes and left.

10

MACE

"Daddy, where are you going?"

Annie saw me throw my bag over my shoulder. I sat on the floor, and all three girls ran over and sat on my lap. I had to force myself not to cry. I love these three so much, but when they would crawl on me, it reminded me of my boys and how they would always wrestle me on the floor. "You said daddies don't leave."

"I'm only going to be gone for a couple of nights. I'm meeting someone in Wyoming. I'm going to get your mommy and bring her here."

"Why? Don't you want us?"

"I will always want you. You and your mommy will stay here with me."

"Are you going to get my mommy out of prison? What about that mean judge? Don't hit him. He'll take you away from us."

"No one will ever take you girls away from your mommy or me. I will call you every day. I want you three to look at me. I love you. You are my life, and I will never leave you."

They threw their arms around me. I didn't realize they

were worried about me leaving them. "Now, let me up so I can bring mommy home." I looked over at my mom. "If you need to drive anywhere, please don't take the girls. I know I'm paranoid, but it's something I can't help right now."

"Honey, I know. We aren't going anywhere, so don't worry about anything. You go and bring their mommy home to them."

I headed out. I would meet up with the president's lawyers in the little town where Hannah lived. They had been looking back on the judges and the public defender's offices, and they would be arrested. They had been making the ladies have sex with them if they wanted to stay out of prison. The first thing I would do was knock both on their asses.

Three hours later, I was driving toward Royal Wyoming. The place was all open spaces. Horses ran along with my rental as I drove down the road. It was pretty in a wild kind of way.

I felt nervous seeing Hannah again. I remembered everything we had done. Neither of us was drunk. So it wasn't because of alcohol that we spent three days together. It was because we didn't want to leave each other. My face felt warm remembering. I don't know why I've had a lot of women since Monica died. I tried not to think about Monica and my boys. It hurt so much, but since the girls have been with me, I remembered the good and funny things I did with the boys, and I would catch myself chuckling.

As I drove through the small town, I saw the police vehicles parked at the small city hall. I knew the lawyers were there and the judge was arrested for all the fraud he created. I parked the car and went inside. I heard shouting as I walked inside. I went straight to the croud that had gathered. The judge looked like he needed to lose some weight.

His face was red and bloated. I could tell he was a drinker, or more like a drunk.

"Who are you?" The judge shouted as he saw me enter the room. "Get him out of here, he's probably with the newspaper."

I looked at the lawyers. "I'm Mason Cohen." I shook their hands. "Are you throwing them in prison?"

"Yes, they'll have a trial, but I can assure you they will go to prison. They will be there for a long time. We found other things that they are involved in."

I walked to where the man stood, and another man was brought into the room. I looked at the policeman and told him to read them their rights. That got some more roars from both of them. "Who the fuck are you?" the judge demanded.

"Mace Cohen. You fucked with the wrong woman."

"What woman is that?"

"Hannah Lial belongs to me, and you upset my girls. For that, you made me angry."

"I don't give a fuck who I made angry. Arrest these people," he yelled to the police.

My fist flew and hit him right in the nose, then I turned and hit the other man. "I'm going to get Hannah. There will be many people you put away set free, and you made me angry, which means the President of the United States is angry. I will let his security take care of this while I get my lady." I don't know why I called her my lady. It was just something I said to shut them up. The girls are my daughters, so I would naturally feel like Hannah was mine. Right?

I drove to the prison and saw people walking out of those big doors. People pulled up in their cars crying when they spotted their family. I saw Hannah walking out. She was beautiful, tall, and graceful. Her long curly hair was wild around her. She wore jeans and cowboy boots. She spotted me and smiled.

Tears ran down her face as she hurried toward me. Her arms went around my waist as I gathered her into my arms. There it was again, my heart started pumping hard and my breathing hitched. I became hard and held her away so she wouldn't feel it. I didn't want to scare her off.

"Thank you for getting us out of prison. I don't know how you did it. I'm just glad you did. I know I was only in there for a week, but it was horrible. I talked to women who the judge put in there for no reason. That bastard, I should have hit him again. How are my babies? I miss them so much."

I opened the truck door for her. "Our babies," I corrected. "They are wonderful. They are with their grandma right now."

"You didn't bring them with you?"

"No, I'm taking you home with me."

"Mace, I can't do that. I have my animals. What am I supposed to do with them? My neighbor won't care for them when I'm out of prison. It was until I got out of prison, no longer. Plus, I have my house."

"Sell it. I want you and the girls to be with me."

"What? Mace, no. I don't even know you. I can't move in with a stranger."

"We are hardly strangers. We have three girls, who I love very much, and I don't want them away from me. Move to Oregon. You'll love it, and they have ranches there. Sell your house, and you can buy one there."

"I can't. I've always lived here. This was my family home. Turn left up here. What would the girls think if I moved them to Oregon?"

"The girls love it there. They love their grandma and me.

Can you stay there for a while and see if you will like it." I looked over at her. She was chewing on her lower lip, thinking, trying to decide what she should do.

"Okay, I can do that. Let me pack a suitcase..." She stopped talking. I looked to see what she was looking at.

"Was that your house?" I asked, looking at a burned-down house.

"Yes. What the heck happened to my house?"

There was a man in the pasture behind the house. When he saw Hannah, he walked over to where she stood, staring at the house and barn.

"Hannah, I'm glad you're out. We don't know how the house and barn burned down. The cows and the pigs didn't make it out of the barn. Your horses are at my place."

"I was gone for a week. How could this happen?"

"The insurance investigator was here. He may know what happened. You'll have to call him."

"Wait, where did you say my horses were?"

I watched Hannah. She looked like she might cry. Her beautiful stormy blue eyes had tears in them.

"I have your horses. I brought them to my property. You can leave them there as long as you want to."

She turned toward me. "My dad gave me my horse, and the others belonged to my brothers. I can't lose them. Sally and Whitney were my cows. Now I don't have them or any of my other animals."

"How about we get a hold of your insurance guy? Then we'll go get the girls."

"Okay... I hate going into town. What if I see the judge?"

"The judge and all of his cohorts are locked up. Don't worry about them." I reached into my pocket, pulled out five hundred dollars, and gave it to the man, "Take good care of Hannah's horses."

"Oh, you better know I will. Thank you."

I drove back to town and walked into the insurance office with Hannah. A woman came out from behind her desk. "Hannah, thank God you are okay. Did you hear what happened with the judge and his nephew? I'm so sorry about your house and barn."

"Yes, I heard. Do you know what happened to my house and barn? Everything I owned was in that house. All of my mama's things."

"The only thing I've been able to figure out is that someone set them on fire."

"But who would do that?"

"Has anyone wanted to buy your property?"

"Yes, the judge asked me if I wanted to sell my property. Do you think he would hire someone to do such a thing?"

"I wouldn't put it past him. I'll deposit you a check so you can start rebuilding."

"Jill Wong, this is Mace Cohen. He's the girls' father."

"I also hear he's friends with the President of the United States."

"I wouldn't call us friends. He owed me a favor, so his investigators checked out the judge. When I told them about Hannah being arrested, his lawyers came here to get the other innocent people out of jail and prison. She slapped the judge for putting his hand where he shouldn't have. He knew about bad judges and he wanted to do something about it."

Hannah looked at me. "Can we go by the bank so I can get another debit card?"

"Of course. Where is it?"

"Turn right at the stop sign. It's the only bank in town. I think I'll start a new bank account in Oregon. I don't trust anyone in this town anymore. I can't wait to see my girls. I just realized these clothes are the same ones I wore when I entered prison."

"I saw a Target on my way from the airport. Why don't we stop there after the bank."

"Thank you. I'm sorry you've been brought into all of this. I know you said we won't ever contact each other, and I wouldn't have contacted you, but I didn't have anyone to watch the girls."

"I was an ass for saying that, so I want you to forget I said any of that. I'm so thankful you found me. I've been all over the country. I settled down when my mom got sick. I was a bastard for not realizing my mom was suffering the same as I was."

"I'm sure you weren't even thinking. You were in a lot of pain."

"So were you. How are you doing?"

"When I realized I was pregnant, I knew God sent me a baby—then there were three. God sent me my girls because he was worried about me. Now all I have are my memories. I don't even have pictures."

"You can take new pictures. I'm scared to put photos of my boys up. I'm afraid I will go back down that black hole."

"I'm sorry." She scooted over and hugged me. I felt my cock come alive. Damn, now was not a good time for him to wake up. She kissed my neck.

"Sorry," she jumped back onto her side. "It's just, you smell so good, I wanted to taste you. I haven't tasted anyone since I was with you. I'm sorry for even talking right now. Forget everything I said."

I pulled off the road and parked. "Hannah, I'm not going to be able to forget you said you wanted to taste me because I want to taste you too. Do you remember how we were when we got together? We both couldn't get enough of each other. How about we get a room?"

"You want me?"

"Damn right, I do."

"If I had been in my right mind when we were together for those three days, I wouldn't have let you go."

"But what about your wife?"

"What about her."

"You love her."

"I did love her." I took a deep breath and ran my hands down my face. I looked at Hannah. "When Monica had the wreck…" I was whispering because I didn't want to say this out loud.

"I have never told anyone what I thought. This can go no further than you and me," I whispered. "She was so depressed. When we got married, she was always quiet; sometimes, she sat on the sofa for hours. I realized she was getting worse. I didn't realize she was chronically depressive."

"When my oldest son was born, she became even more depressed. My mom was helping her a lot because I was away more than I should have been. I was in the Navy Seals. That was going to be my life. When my other son, Anthony, was born, my mother was concerned about Monica being alone with the boys. When Anthony was three, my mom thought Monica was getting depressed again.

"She thought Monica might be bipolar or something. She called me, but I was too late. They were all gone. The train hit the car and killed all three of them." I didn't realize I was crying until Hannah wiped the tears from my face. "I believe she parked the car on the track when she saw the train…" I growled in a whisper as she rested her forehead against mine.

"Oh, no. Fuck. Now I understand why you were so miserable. You feel you should have been home."

"Don't you think I should have been? My boys were five and three. They were old enough to know that train would hit them."

"How could you have known this would happen? Nobody knows what another person is going to do. You couldn't watch her every minute of the day. We do what we can in this world to survive. We take care of our family the best we can. I wonder if your mom also thought that's what happened."

"I've thought she might have had that same thought as me. She had a heart attack. When I was drunk with grief, I remember her telling me that she shouldn't have let them stay with Monica."

"So she blamed herself as much as you did."

"God, I hope not… I feel like a ton of weight has been taken off my chest because I told you my thoughts."

"I will never repeat what you told me."

"I know you won't. Can we stay together tonight and leave tomorrow?"

"I would love to stay with you tonight."

I kissed her lips, and then I started the vehicle back up.

Hannah reached over and took my hand. I picked her hand up. "We'll get a room near the airport."

"Okay, do you think I'm a little crazy for telling you how good you smell and that I want to taste you? I mean, who says that to someone who just got them out of prison? And to top it off, I haven't seen you in four years. Please tell me if you think I am crazy. I tend to say anything when I'm nervous."

I chuckled, "I think I'm going to pull over if you tell me that again." She laughed and scooted closer to me.

We got a room at the Marriott. I was so nervous as if it was my first time. We went up in the elevator. I took Hannah's hand in mine and drew her closer to me. When we got to our room, she looked at me.

"Are we doing the right thing, making love? You know, once we start, we won't want to stop. I'm going to shower first. I just came out of prison."

"Okay." I stripped out of my clothes while Hannah was in the shower. When I stepped inside with her, she smiled.

"You're still as beautiful as I remember. Maybe a few more tattoos."

I chuckled. "Wait, that was what I was going to say. You look beautiful. I remember how soft your body was. It's still like silk. Let me wash you."

"Okay, I'm in your hands to do whatever you want with me."

"I love those words, so don't be surprised if I keep you up all night." I lathered my hands up with soap and started washing her. My hands trailed over her breast and down between her thighs.

She whispered my name softly like a feather falling from the sky. My mouth devoured hers, and she cried out when I slipped my fingers between her folds. The noises from her made it hard not to push inside her right now. I was throbbing to enter her, But first, I wanted to make her orgasm. My thumb played with her clit as my fingers pleasured her. She climaxed, and her body shook.

She looked at me, and I picked her up, and she wrapped her legs around me as I entered her. She threw her head back and watched me as I pounded in and out of her. I was ready to orgasm. I looked at her, and she called my name as she orgasmed. A second later, I released deep inside her. We laughed as I lifted her and carried her to the bed. I ripped the covers off and laid her down.

My tongue explored her mouth before it nibbled her neck and ear lobe. I took a breast into my mouth and then the other. Her body fit mine perfectly.

When I entered her, she cried out for all of it. I raised and pushed inside her. She cried out my name. We were like lovers that have been separated forever. I came at the same time Hannah did.

I rested my elbows on the bed with my forehead resting on hers. "Damn, you're good. You're so tight for me. Do you feel me? I'm ready for you again."

"Then do it. I'm ready for you too. I want to do it all night and into the morning until our plane leaves."

I chuckled. "I told you how we were together; we can last forever."

"Yes, we can," she said, pushing her body to meet mine.

Around three, we were both sweaty and worn out. Even though I still throbbed for her, it was time to take a break. "Let's get some sleep," I said, pulling her up next to me. She was asleep almost immediately.

I woke up. Hannah was still sleeping, so I was quiet as I got out of bed and went to the shower.

Five minutes later, she entered. We made love as if it was our last time together.

"What time does our plane leave?"

"We have three hours."

"I need to buy some clothes."

"Are you saying you'll cover up this beautiful body?"

"Yes, unfortunately, that's what I'm saying."

"I better take advantage of it before you do that."

"Yes, I was hoping you would say that."

11

GILLY

This place is beautiful. The coffee shop was on the pier. I opened the windows, and the breeze felt like heaven. The décor was coming along beautifully. I went with shabby chic because I love shabby chic. The previous owner sold me all the equipment, and I made an agreement to have all of the pastries brought here every morning with the donut shop in town.

I heard a vehicle and looked out the window. I smiled as my friend, Rene, walked inside. "Oh, Gilly, it's beautiful. I love your colors. They are perfect. When are you opening?"

"In the morning. I can't wait. I'm so excited and nervous."

"I can't believe I'm moving right when you move to my town."

"I know. I wish you didn't have to move away. I hope I learned all I need to know from my classes."

"Are you kidding me, Gillian Marshall? You were at the top of your class in everything. You'll be great. I mean, you gave up a six-million-dollar-a-year job to make coffee for angry people."

Men will buy coffee all day, so they can look at the beautiful woman who purchased the coffee shop. Plus, you have the apartment over the shop. I still can't believe you are here.

"This is a perfect spot. I come here every morning for my coffee and pastries. I'm glad you're keeping the pastries. My favorite is the donuts with the chocolate. Anyway, I must get to work and see you in the morning. Why don't you come to our house for dinner Saturday night? We will celebrate you opening your shop."

"I would love that. What time should I show up?"

"Come at six, and we'll eat, and then we will party. Not that I party much anymore. You'll have to be up and have my coffee for me at six-thirty.

I chuckled. "I'll get up at five, start the coffee machines, and pray I know what I'm doing."

My alarm didn't go off when it was supposed to. I had planned on arriving early; it was five thirty, and I had to open at six. I flew out of bed and dressed so fast I forgot my shoes. I put my hair on top of my head. Someone was knocking at the door. I opened it with an apology on my lips and froze.

"Gilly, what are you doing here?"

"What are you doing here?"

"This is my town."

"I bought the coffee shop." I looked at him and started crying.

He stepped inside and put his arms around me. "Why are you crying?"

"My alarm didn't go off, and I'm late. I haven't even started the coffee. This is my first day. I missed you."

"I'll help you. I missed you too. I haven't seen you in almost a year." He had a big grin as he looked at me, "Did you know this was my hometown? Is that why you bought this coffee shop? You wanted to surprise me."

"No. My friend, Rene, lives here, and I always heard her talking about Cedar Falls, Oregon. I can't believe you live here."

He laughed loudly, picked me up, and swung me around in a circle. When he set me down, he kissed me. I threw my arms around him and kissed him back. "I have to get this coffee made. I don't want to screw my first day up."

"I'll help you."

"Do you know how?"

"Yes, this was Aunt Betty's shop. I used to work here some weekends back when I was a teenager." Gray smiled and shook his head. "I can't believe you moved to my town." He talked as he worked. I was busy getting things ready in another pot.

"I went to your work, and they told me you broke up with your fiancé and quit your job."

"You went to my work?"

"Yes, I wanted to take you back to the ship. So you broke up with him?"

"Well, I couldn't be with one man when I had just had the best sex in my life with another man."

"Are you telling me that night we were together was the best sex in your life? Wow, I hope tonight lives up to your expectations."

"I'm sure it will," I said, grinning. He reached for me and kissed me again. He was still kissing me when I heard the bell over the door. Gray turned and guarded me with his back, blocking me from my first customer. I stepped around him, and Gabe stood there. "Hi, Gabe."

"How did you know Gray lived here? This is amazing." He ordered his coffee and two donuts.

"I didn't know Gray lived here. I moved here because my friend lives here—Rene."

"Rene Woody? She's my cousin."

"That's crazy," I laughed. I was happy until the next person walked inside. I smiled at her. She walked past me and put her arms around Gray. She kissed him before he moved her arms and stepped away from her.

"Sharon, this is Gilly Marshall. I told you about her.

"What can I get for you, Sharon?"

"I want a regular coffee. I don't like all that weird stuff people put in their coffee."

I gave her coffee to her, and she left. I turned to Gray. "Was she your girlfriend? I didn't move here to break you and your girlfriend up. I didn't even know you lived here."

"I have only one girlfriend, and her name is Gilly Marshall. I don't know why Sharon kissed me like that. It'll never happen again."

"I'm glad I picked this town to live in. If you need to go to work, I'll be fine here by myself."

"I wish I could stay with you but I have to go."

"I'll see you later."

"Yes, you will."

There were a lot of people who came in to see who the new owner of The Coffee Shop was. I have never seen so many moms with little ones. It was like everyone had a child at the same time. I knew I was going to love this little town with so many friendly people in it.

I smiled all day. I closed at five. It was a long day. I was busy the entire time. I cleaned everything. I had just finished cleaning when Gray walked back in. I smiled as he pulled me into his arms.

"We don't know a lot about each other. Maybe we should get to know each other. Are you still doing deep sea rescues?"

"No, we are now Seals Security. We have a lot of Seals working with us. We have done a couple of deep-sea rescues, but it's not something I want to do anymore. What about you? You were like what; a famous engineer for the big oil rigs? Now you own a little coffee shop in a beach town."

"I took some time off to decide what I wanted to do. I've always wanted some kind of business where I wasn't working seven days a week."

"You picked the wrong business. This coffee shop has always stayed open seven days a week. My Aunt worked all the time."

"Yes, she told me that after I bought it. I'm going to find someone to work with me. Follow me," I whispered, leading the way upstairs. As soon as we shut the door, I took my top off. "I've had dreams about you. Lots of them. Do you think I'm moving too fast? Am I too pushy? I can slow down if you want."

"Hell no, you're reading my mind. I've had so many dreams of you. Do you think I'm crazy because we don't really know each other that much?"

"No, if you're crazy, then so am I. So you don't have a crazy bone in your body. I knew we would find each other again. I'm glad it only took ten months instead of another eight years." I reached up and pulled his shirt over his head as he backed me into the bedroom. He had us naked while still kissing me. We fell on the bed laughing. "I missed you, Gray."

"I missed you too, sweetheart. I'm keeping you here with me forever." He held my face and kissed me long and hard. "This first time will be hot and fast because I need you now."

"Take me, Gray. I need you too."

"Do you want this?"

"Yes," I replied, breathlessly. "I want this. I want you. All of you." My body was sizzling in anticipation. Gray loosened his grip on me, and I slid down his hot, slick body until his pulsing hard on was pressed tightly against my belly, and when he entered me, I cried out his name.

His hands sank into my thighs while his lips devoured mine. He trailed hot kisses down my throat, sucking and licking the length of it. All the time, he slid his body up and down. His hard erection went deep inside of me, moving fast. I orgasmed two times before he jerked against me, sending heat pouring into me. Never in a thousand years would I have thought I might like sex a little rough. But I wanted him to take me hard and fast, again.

I looked into his eyes. "Gray," I whispered into his chest. I couldn't help the tremble in my voice. Being held in his arms, I knew I had found my place in this world, and it was right here in bed with this man.

"I want you so much it scares me, Gilly. You are mine forever. I finally have you after all this time."

He inhaled my scent. I must have smelled pretty good because he bit my neck. I almost climaxed; it felt so good. Then he was moving again. He took it slower as his kisses trailed down my neck to my breast. It felt like I was wrapped around a giant, beautiful vibrator that had Mace's lovely hot smell when we made love on the ship. Gray was all man. He smelled so damn good I licked him.

"Did you just lick me?" he chuckled.

"Yes, you smell so good I wanted to bite you, but I didn't think you would like that," I giggled. Then I purred deep in my throat. He was making me have orgasm after orgasm the way he was making love to me. "I can't wait to get to know you." I knew that sounded crazy when he chuckled against my neck.

"What if you don't like me?"

"That would never happen because I already like you a lot." I swear I purred again, the noise coming from me. I had never made love like this before. I was flooded with hot, slick desire.

"Hold tight," he whispered. I didn't have time to answer, his hands slipped under my bottom, and he thrust deeper inside my slick folds. I came instantly. I screamed his name and clawed his back as the aftershocks battered my body. It wasn't long before my body was craving his again. The need rolled inside of me for more.

"Gilly, I need you. I'm struggling to stay in control, darling."

"Gray, let go and lose control," I replied. "Make love to me like you want to."

Immediately, he grasped my thighs and raised me to the length of his erection. He gripped my thighs and pulled my hips down, pushing himself deeper inside me. I was so high on desire I couldn't think or speak. All I could do was feel. I couldn't even remember my name.

"Let go, my sweet. I've got you," he murmured into my ear.

I looked up into his face. Something shimmered in his eyes. I wasn't sure what it was. I found my release. I screamed his name as my body spasmed in ecstasy.

For several minutes we remained like that. We would've been unable to move if we had wanted to. My ragged breathing calmed, and I relaxed against Gray's chest. Resting my head on his chest, I listened to his rapidly beating heart, enjoying that he had been just as affected by our lovemaking as I had been. My hand splayed across the muscles above his heart, my thumb idly brushing his skin. His words replayed in my mind. *'I've got you,'* he'd said. And in that perfect moment, I trusted that he did have me. I went to sleep. When I woke up, Gray watched me. He was propped up on his elbow.

"How long have I been asleep?"

"A couple of hours. Are you hungry?"

"I'm starving. I'll shower, then make us something. I'm a pretty good cook."

"I'll shower with you, and then we will cook together."

"That sounds even better," I said, kissing his shoulder.

12

GRAY

I've had two weeks of the hottest sex in my life. I had to go away for a while; I didn't want to. I wanted to stay with Gilly and never leave her. I walked into the coffee shop, and she was closing. She smiled when she saw me.

"Why do you look so sad?" Gilly asked, looking at me.

"I have to go away for a few weeks. I don't want to be away from you that long."

"I'm going to miss you. When are you going?"

"Tomorrow."

"Well, there you go. We have all night for each other." I pulled her to me and kissed her long and thoroughly.

"You make me happy." I wanted to say I love you because I did love her, but I didn't want to scare her away from me.

"You make me happy too. I told Rene I would have dinner with them tonight. I'll call her and tell her you are leaving tomorrow."

"No, I'll go with you. Rene will think I don't want to share you," I chuckled.

"She would be right; I'm not particularly eager to share you. But we'll have tonight."

GRAYSON

~

WE WERE TAKING the two men we were guarding to a different place. This was the third place we'd moved them to. They had made some mean people angry. Thomas, one of the men we were guarding, called the police on his neighbor for beating up his daughter. The man thought he could do anything he wanted to her since she was his daughter.

The police arrested him and had an ambulance take the daughter to the hospital. She had many broken bones. The other man, Richard, slugged the man in the face when he went crazy and hit Thomas for calling the police.

The man who was from Iran had some men come for Richard and Thomas, who were a couple. They almost killed him. I looked at Thomas. He didn't look that healthy. "I think you should get some x-rays. You might have a punctured lung. We'll go to a hospital in this state. The Iranians don't know where we are. I'll run you in for some x-rays, and then we'll return to Richard's location. You have to be checked out."

"Yes, I agree," Richard said. "You have to go. I'll stay right here. You'll be in and out in no time at all."

"Okay, but I will not stay in the hospital if they want to keep me."

"Okay, let's go. Your hair is a different color. You aren't using anything that has your name on it. You'll be fine. I won't leave your side. You won't have anything to worry about."

We jumped into the SUV and drove down the mountain into town. "When they ask your name, tell them what we agreed on. Do you remember that name?"

"Joe Black. How could I forget? Brad Pitt was so hot in

that movie. I swear Richard was jealous for a month over me drooling over that man," he chuckled. "Did you notice the look Richard gave you? Oh yeah, he was jealous."

I laughed out loud. "I wondered what was wrong with Richard."

"Why would a father beat his daughter so severely that her bones are broken?"

"Those people are different from us. They think they have the right to kill their daughters if they aren't doing what they should, according to what they want them to do. We know it's not right, and I hope he rots in hell for hurting his daughter the way he did. Do you know why he said he beat her?"

"No," Thomas said, shaking his head. "Do you?"

"Yes, because she refused to marry his friend. The man is sixty years old. His daughter is fifteen."

"He's a bastard," Thomas snarled. "No one in the neighborhood liked him. He was always treating his wife like she was a dog. They would walk the block, and she had to walk behind him. She was frightened to death of him."

"Maybe she will leave him. Here we are. What's your name?"

"Joe Black. She won't leave him. She thinks whatever he does to them, they must deserve it."

"That's a shame. Okay, Joe, let's get this done."

I walked behind Thomas as he walked into the hospital. I talked to the head of security, and we were immediately taken back to get an x-ray. We were out of there in an hour. I stopped at CVS to pick up Thomas's meds. He had two broken ribs. They wrapped his ribs, and he also had an infection in his lungs, so he got some antibiotics.

Richard met us in the garage. He looked like he was distraught. We explained what was going on, and then we went inside. Gabe was cooking dinner. My mind went to Gilly, and I smiled.

"Dinner is ready."

I walked into the living room and told the guys dinner was ready. Richard was on the phone. I stopped and looked at him. "Who were you talking to?" I asked, barking each word out so he would know I was pissed. They weren't supposed to have phones.

"Myrtle. I had to let her know what is going on. I promised her I would."

"Eat your dinner. After you eat, pack your bags. We can't take a chance that Myrtle won't tell someone where we are."

Thomas walked into the room carrying his plate. He looked at Richard, "What have you done? Do you want to bring those men to us? How many times have you talked to Myrtle?"

"I've only called her when we move to a different place. I promised to keep her informed."

"I can't believe you. Get your shit packed. We'll drop you off at the bus station on our way to another spot. I will not tell you where we are. I don't want you with me anymore."

I hurried and ate my dinner while the guys packed their things in their room. Richard cried, begging Thomas to let him go with us. I thought it would be safer to take Richard with us, so I decided. I walked into their room. Richard will go with us. "Please give me your phone." He handed over the phone, and I busted it. "I don't want to take a chance that this phone has been tracked. Now, eat. We need to leave."

"If he comes with us, I will not talk to him. I'm so angry that he didn't think about me before he called that gossip monger Myrtle. What am I saying? He's as bad as she is. Why I stayed with him this long, I have no idea. Well, no more."

I walked into the other room where Gabe was eating his dinner. He was snickering. "What are you smirking about?"

"You. You are always in the middle of people's lives. What I mean is couples. I bet you one hundred dollars that before this night ends, you'll be counseling them."

"You're crazy. Who did I counsel?"

"You tried counseling Ryker when Janet ran off with her boss. But he told you to go screw yourself."

"I wasn't trying to counsel him. I told him he was better off knowing she was a bitch before he married her. He was pissed at me for telling him the truth. He didn't want to hear it. Everything I told him was the truth, and he knew it. She thought she could snap her fingers, and he would come running back her again. She's a bitch. I knew how she was in high school."

"If I remember right, you went out with her several times."

"That's how I knew she was a bitch. Let's get out of here."

13

GILLY

I was up earlier than usual, so I tried my hand at making ham and egg on an English muffin. It was delicious. I've been trying to add more to the menu. Something that was quick and easy but tasted good. I started writing down what other things I could put on the menu.

I started making the coffee when the door opened. I looked up, and Lucy stood there smiling. I screamed and ran to her. We hugged each other.

"What are you doing here?"

"I came for a visit."

"Where are the children?"

"They are with their dads. That doesn't sound very nice. My three kids are with their three dads. And now I'm single."

"What happened?"

"I just admitted to myself I loved Adam too much to be with another man. It wasn't fair to either of us, but mainly to the man I was married to. I had to force myself to have sex with them. I would close my eyes and pretend it was Adam, and he still loved me. I'm an idiot. So I'm here to visit you. Mom eloped with John, our sheriff."

"What? Mom eloped. When was this?"

"The day after you left. Now they are on a trip abroad. They said they might stay there for six months or more."

"I'm so happy you are here with me. Let me make you something to eat. Pour yourself a cup of coffee."

I saw Lucy looking around. "It's beautiful. I love your decorations. I remember how you loved shabby chic. I had her sit down while I made an egg and ham English muffin. Here you go. Oh, my pastries are here."

"These look delicious. Does the bakery make them every morning.?"

"Yes, take one and tell me what you think."

"Yummy... They melt in my mouth."

"I know. I love it here. The town is so pretty. Everyone is so friendly."

My first customer came in, and I was busy most of the morning. Every time I looked at Lucy, she was visiting with the people in the shop. I smiled, knowing how she must be missing her kids. Lucy never went anywhere without her babies.

There was a break in customers, so I sat next to Lucy. I smiled as I watched her. You look beautiful today. Lucy always looked beautiful. I always thought of her as someone who had a beautiful soul. She was good to every person she met. Everyone loved her.

"Tell me why your heart hurts?"

"You always could do that. All you had to do was look at me, and you would know what I was feeling." A tear rolled down her face. "I heard Adam was getting married. My heart is broken. I'm a broken woman, and I don't know if I'll ever be unbroken."

"He wouldn't fight for me. He didn't even try to change his ways. He picked his father and those bikers over me. Was I supposed to raise my children with all those bikers at my home? It's been five years. I've married two other men, and he still hasn't fought for me."

"Maybe he thinks you don't love him because you've married two other men."

"Adam knows I love him. He knows he's the only man I will ever love. I just feel so broken. He told me he would never love another woman."

"Why don't I close early, and we'll take a walk on the beach? Wait, do you still surf?"

"Yes, I do."

"Let's go surfing. You can wear one of my swimsuits."

"Are you sure you want to do that?"

"Yes, you know I only wanted to work three days a week. I need to hire some help so I can take time off when I want. You'll never believe who lives in this town."

"Is it someone I went to school with?"

"No."

"Is it someone I know?"

"No."

"Then tell me. Who is it?"

"My wrong date."

"What? Did you know he lived here?"

"No. He walked in through that door for a cup of coffee and a donut," I said, pointing at the front door. "And I could have fallen over. He's away on a job right now. He and his buddies have a Navy Seal security business."

"I am so happy for you. Now you really know it was fate that brought you here."

"Yes, now I know. Let's go surfing."

I laughed so hard I swallowed a mouth full of salt water.

Lucy was doing handstands on the surfboard we rented. She was outstanding. I remember she and Adam surfed every day after school. She taught the big tough Adam how to surf. Lucy told me they made love every night in high school. Adam was a senior, and Lucy was a sophomore. She would say they couldn't keep their hands off each other. Now, look at her; she didn't fool me one bit. Lucy was always the clown, mostly when she tried to keep the tears inside.

"Are you choking?" Lucy said, watching me cough.

"I swallowed salt water. This is fun. I'm so happy we decided to surf."

"Me too. I'm worn out. It's been so long since I've surfed. Let's find something to eat. I hear these restaurants have excellent seafood."

"They do. Let's go home and shower, and then we'll come back and eat." We returned the surfboards and then walked home. We went through the small town, it was so pretty. We walked in the back entrance to my apartment above my coffee shop. It was a beautiful day. Having Lucy there made it even nicer.

~

We sat in a popular restaurant when I felt someone staring at me. I looked around and didn't see anyone, so I continued eating my lobster tail.

"This food is delicious. Man, whoever their cook is, I would hang on to them. I'm in love with the sauce. I wonder if I could get the recipe."

"You'll never know if you will get the recipe without asking."

"After we eat, I'll ask. It's a beautiful place to live. I'm thinking about moving. I can't live in the same town as Adam and his new wife."

"Why don't you move here? I would love to live near you and the girls. Will their fathers try and stop you from moving away?"

"I have full custody of my girls. I can do whatever I want to do. I'll check the hospital and see if they are hiring."

I looked at her and wanted to cry. She was broken, and I couldn't fix her. I reached over and held her hand.

"I'll be alright."

"Was Adam with other women after you left him?"

"Not the first year after I left. After I married Mike, I would see him with women. It was like a knife stabbing me in the heart. Our relationship became different after his dad moved back to town. Then the bikers started showing up at our house. Adam's father was a woman's man, every woman he could get. He would bring two at a time to our home sometimes. I tried talking to Adam about it, but he didn't want his dad to disappear again, so he wouldn't say anything to him."

"That sure wasn't fair to you and Layla. She must have been a baby at the time."

"She was three months when Jack moved back to town. I put up with their crap for three years. One night, I came home from work, and Jack was sleeping on the living room floor with two women. Of course, Adam said how sorry he was. Layla was in our room again. Adam always kept a close eye on her. That wasn't the first time. I would come home after working twelve hours at the hospital, and there would be a bunch of bikers parked out front of our home."

"I'm sorry you went through that. I just can't believe Adam let that happen. He must have changed when his dad moved back to town."

"Yeah, he did. When his mom died while he was still at school, he seemed different. Once, he told me she was murdered. I don't know why he thought that. Jack left when Adam was twelve."

"You did the right thing moving out. That is no place to raise a child. Did you marry Mike to make him jealous?"

"I thought he would come and get me before I got married. Pretty stupid, right? He never showed up at the wedding. So I can't live in the same town as him and his wife. I need to start my life over without wondering what Adam is doing."

"I want you to move here. We will have so much fun. The girls will love it here. Put your house up for sale. I'll call a moving company to move your stuff up here. Why don't we do that on Tuesday?"

"Are you sure?"

"Yes. I'm more than sure."

"I'll talk to the hospital tomorrow."

"Yes. That's a great idea."

"I'll close the coffee shop and put a sign on the door."

14

GRAY

Those two hadn't stopped arguing since they climbed into the vehicle. My headache was getting bigger. I looked over at Gabe. He was sleeping. I stepped on my brakes, and he jerked awake, and the two in the back stopped fighting. "I will make you walk if you don't stop arguing." I looked at Gabe, "I need you to wake up before I kill them two."

"I'm awake. You two need to sleep before Grayson kills all of us."

"I have another headache."

"Did you go to the doctor like you were supposed to?"

"No. Gilly moved to town, and everything went out of my head. I'll call him when we get back home."

Gabe glanced my way. "How much further do we have to drive tonight?"

"Not far."

"How much longer do you think it'll take them to find the girls father?"

"It's already been two weeks. I hope it's not much longer.

I will call Gilly in the morning and talk to her. That will make me fill better."

"Are you feeling sick?"

"No, it's the headache." I wasn't sure Gabe believed me. He kept watching me as I drove to another one of our safe houses. This one was in the mountains out of Bend, Oregon. I cracked my window to let in some fresh air. The night smelled good. It smelled like it had just rained.

I pulled into the driveway, and we all headed inside. Someone was there. The door was wide open. I motioned for the guys to get behind me and proceeded into the house. I couldn't see anyone, but I heard something. I looked at Gabe, and he looked at me simultaneously. We both quickly realized the noise was a bear. "Get back into the vehicle," I whispered to the two men. They backed away and got into the car when the bear came charging.

I slammed the front door, and Gabe and I ran and jumped into the car. I couldn't find the damn keys. Then I realized they were in the car. We were backing out of the driveway when we saw the bear break down the front door. He was huge. I started honking the horn and flashing my lights, and he ran into the forest. We sat there briefly before I pulled back into the driveway.

Gabe opened his car door. "We'll have to see if there is any wood we can block up the front door. There doesn't look to be much left of it."

I looked around, making sure the bear wasn't coming back. "I think there is some plywood in the garage. I hope the inside isn't torn up." It wasn't that bad inside. Some things were knocked over and some broken lamps. I checked the garage. There was a stack of wood. I got a sheet of plywood and carried it to the front door. Next, I went hunting for a hammer and nails. Thirty minutes later, the front door was all boarded up.

"Bedtime," I said, walking to a bedroom. The good thing with the safe houses was they were all large, four bedrooms and over. I would run into town in the morning and load up on groceries.

The following morning, there were no bars on my phone, so I wasn't able to call Gilly. When I went to town, everyone came with me. They were worried the bear would come back. We got groceries, and I tried calling Gilly again.

I still had no bars, so I headed back to the cabin. It was a beautiful drive. If I weren't here working, I would love to walk around town. I used to come here all the time as a teenager with friends to ski.

I had some maintenance to do on the cabin that would keep me busy for a few days. I got some Aleve when I was in town for my headache. I hoped like hell it helped take it away. I wondered what Gilly was doing.

15

GILLY

We were packing some of Lucy's essential things. The realtor put the for sale sign up in her front yard. There's been a lot of tears from Lucy. She grew up in this town. She thought she would always be here with Adam raising their family together. But she needed a change in her life. Lucy couldn't stay in this town watching Adam and his wife grow a family. The woman he's marrying is used to the bikers. Her family is bikers.

She told her second and third husbands about her move but didn't tell Adam. Lucy couldn't bring herself to talk to him. So when he dropped Layla off today and saw the for-sale sign, he flipped. Layla was hugging her mommy when Adam walked inside. He saw the boxes.

"What the fuck is going on? Where are you moving to? It better be around here somewhere."

"Layla, go get your doll."

"To Cedar Falls, Oregon," I said. I looked over at Lucy, and she refused to look at him.

"Look at me, damn it?" She still wouldn't look at him. "Why are you leaving town?"

She was packing when she talked to him. "Because I can't be here anymore."

"Why can't you? Is it because you're getting another divorce?"

"No. That's not why."

"Then tell me."

Finally, she looked at him and tears fell from her eyes. "I can't live in the same town as you and your wife. You promised me that you would love me forever. You wouldn't fight for me. Each time I told you I was engaged, you never did anything. You never fought for me. You've broken me. My heart is torn to shreds. I can't breathe anymore. I can't stay here and watch you marry another woman."

"Why not? I watched you marry two fucking men. I stayed in this town and watched you marry twice."

"You were supposed to fight for me. But I guess that was stupid of me to think you would do something like that. You didn't even choose Layla and me over your dad and all those bikers. Goodbye, Adam."

"Wait, are you fucking telling me you got engaged so I would fight for you? That's the biggest load of bullshit I've ever heard. You can't blame me for you marrying two different men. You are the one who broke yourself. I don't want my daughter to move to another state. I'll get a court order to keep her here if necessary."

"I have full custody of Layla because of the bikers at your house. So don't even try to threaten me with going to court."

"No!" he shouted. "You can't move away."

"I have to. I can't stay here."

I watched as he ran his fingers through his hair. "Only

you would become engaged and marry someone just to get me to fight for you. Why didn't you say something?"

"What could I say? Goodbye." Lucy turned to leave, but Adam grabbed her hand.

"Don't move away. I need you here where I can see you are okay."

"You can visit Layla whenever you want, but you can't bring your wife."

I watched as he pulled Lucy to him, took her face in his hands, and his fingers dug into her hair. His lips kissed her. He devoured her lips. I turned around and walked into the kitchen so they had privacy. A tear slipped from my eye. They loved each other so much but were too pig-headed to fix it.

I returned to the family room and hugged my sister, who was crying so hard my heart was breaking for both of them. "Why don't you fight for Adam? He didn't know you wanted him to fight for you, but you could fight for him."

"How?"

"Go over there and tell that woman that Adam belongs to you. We'll be here for a week. He loves you. I know he does."

"What if I make a fool of myself?"

"So what! Make a fool of yourself. If nothing else, he'll know how you feel, and so will his fiancée."

"I'll go in the morning. My emotions couldn't handle it anymore today. I have to meet with the movers. They'll be here soon."

I watched as she walked to the sofa and sat down. I sat beside her and put my arm around her. Layla came out of her room with her dolls.

"What's wrong with Mommy?"

"She's going to be okay. Have you had lunch? Why don't we make some sandwiches?"

"Yeah, peanut butter and jelly."

"We got up and went into the kitchen.

∽

WE LOOKED AROUND AND SMILED. "Okay, we will have three weeks to find you a home. But if we don't, you can still stay with me. Have you decided if you are going to fight for Adam?"

"Yes, I have. We are going to stop and let Layla tell her daddy goodbye. And I've decided I'm going to tell him goodbye also."

We were driving to Oregon, so we were all in Lucy's SUV. I stayed in the car as they said their goodbyes. Then I thought I should get out and see what was going on. The door was open, and Adam hugged Layla as his girlfriend stood close by his side. She surprised me. She wore her makeup heavily on her face. Her clothes were leather pants and a skimpy tank top. She didn't look anything like Lucy, who was more the girl next door, especially with her blue jean shorts and her cute button-up shirt.

Adam put Layla down and looked at Lucy. "Goodbye, Lucy."

"Goodbye."

Before I knew what Lucy would do, she stepped close to Adam, took his face in her hands, and kissed him. Lucy kissed him as he had kissed her a few days back. When she stepped back, I saw her lips tremble. I knew Adam had also seen her lips tremble. He took a step toward her, but his girlfriend grabbed his arm.

"There, that was me fighting back. You know she will

start in on him as soon as we leave. Let's go pick up my other girls. I'm so glad I made this decision. I can't wait to find a home for me and my girls."

We stopped and spent the night in Mendocino so the girls could stretch their legs. I carried the baby as we walked on the beach. I heard a car peeling out and looked around when I heard a horn honking. I saw a white truck speeding down the road.

For some reason, it made me uneasy. I didn't have time to dwell on that because the baby wanted all my attention. Grace was so precious. All three of Lucy's girls were special. Lucy lived her life for her girls. I wish I could do something for Lucy and Adam, but they had to do it for themselves.

When we drove through Cedar Falls, I was so happy I lived here it was beautiful. The coffee shop was opened. How did that happen? We climbed out of the vehicle and walked inside the building. I smiled at the woman making coffee and chatting with a couple sitting at the counter.

"Betty, what are you doing here?"

"I had a call that the shop was closed. I knew you were hunting for help, and I missed this place so much. Can I be the help you are looking for?"

"Heck yeah, you can. How many days a week do you want to work?"

"Three."

"That's perfect. I want to work three also, so we can close on Sunday. We'll work out our days, and if we have to change them, we will. We'll also hire someone to help during the day. This is my sister, Lucy. She starts working at the hospital on Monday. Lucy is a nurse, and she's moving here where I am."

"That's wonderful. I bet you two are worn out. How would you like a nice mocha frappe?"

"Yummy, I want one," Lucy said.

"Me too," I said as I moved Gracie to my other hip. She was only six months old but growing fast, and I loved her. We got our drinks and took them upstairs. Then we used the back door to bring in the suitcases.

"I'm glad I did this. I already feel like I can breathe again. Thank you for helping me," Lucy said.

"Of course, I helped you. You're my sister, and I love you."

"I love you too."

16

GRAY

When I went for groceries, I called Gilly. "Hello."

"Gray, I'm so happy you called. Guess what? Lucy has moved here. She sold her home and moved here where I live. She's bought a house down the street from yours. It's her and her three baby girls. I wish you were here. I'm on this giant emotional roller coaster. I swear you should have seen Lucy and Adam. They still love each other so much, but both of them are pigheaded. When are you coming back?"

"Probably in a few days. I miss you."

"I miss you too. I have so much to tell you. Guess who is helping me with the shop?"

"I think it's Aunt Betty."

"How did you know?"

"I knew she wouldn't be able to stay still long. So this works out for both of you."

"Yes, she's so sweet. She told me if the shop looked like this, she would never have left. I'm glad she likes the décor.

"Look, I can't talk long. I have to get back. I'll call you

when I'm on my way home. I can't wait to hold you in my arms again."

"I can't wait either. Be careful, Grayson."

"I will, sweetheart."

I wanted to tell her I loved her. But the first time wouldn't be over the phone.

When I got back to the cabin, it was empty. *Where the hell is everyone? Fuck, what the hell happened?* I took out my gun and walked into the forest as quietly as possible. I looked around. I heard someone stepping on leaves. They weren't very quiet.

"Run, Gray," Gabe said.

I ran toward the noise. If I caught them off guard, I could kill them before they could kill me. I heard Gabe running toward me as well. So when I saw the Iranians in front of me, I fired. *Two down. How many are there?*

I saw a movement out of the corner of my eye and turned my head; it was Gabe. I signed that there were two down, and he signed two up. So we had two of them out here somewhere still. I changed directions. "Where are Thomas and Richard?" I mumbled under my breath. I heard footsteps and hit the ground while Gabe fired his gun. He killed one of them. A bullet landed close to me. I turned over and fired. The last one fell.

I got up and looked at Gabe. "How the hell did they find us?"

"Is there a GPS on our vehicle? Let's pull it into the garage and check it out."

"Where are Thomas and Richard?"

"In the attic."

"Fuck, I hope there is no GPS on our vehicle. Because if there is, one of them put it on our truck." I drove the vehicle into the garage and checked under the truck.

"Here it is," Gabe said, standing up with the GPS.

We went inside and called them down. While Gabe called them down, I called Ryker. "Hey, we killed four men. We had a GPS under our vehicle. It had to be one of the guys we're guarding." I Gave him more information, and he was going to get hold of the authorities. When I walked back inside, Thomas was choking Richard.

"He got paid one hundred thousand dollars to put that on our vehicle."

"Get him off of me. I only did it because I knew you would kill them. I knew we were all safe."

I pulled him away from Thomas and cuffed him with zip ties.

"You can't cuff me. You don't have the authority to do this. Take these off of me, right now."

"So, it wasn't Myrtle you were talking to. No wonder you wanted to come with us. You pretended it was because you were worried about Thomas." We heard the sirens as four cop cars pulled onto the property.

"I was worried about Thomas. Don't leave me here."

I talked to the police and walked them to where the bodies were. I told them everything Richard did. "Whatever you do, don't let him out. If he wants to call his lawyer, listen in on the conversation."

"He won't get anything. We'll keep him locked up. We might even misplace him for a month or two."

"Thanks." Gabe packed our bags, and we left. Thomas didn't say a word. I knew he was in shock because he had pleaded for us to let Richard come along.

So, we were off to another safe house. This one was in Florence, Oregon, along the river. I enjoyed this safe house because I fished here. The groceries were still in the vehicle. "Thomas, can you hand me one of those apples from the grocery bag? Help yourself to whatever you want in those bags. There are some candy bars in there."

"I'm sorry, you guys. I can't believe that bastard did that. Is my life only worth one hundred thousand to him? I hope he gets killed in jail. I have more money than I can ever spend. Why would he do that?"

"Does Richard have money?"

"I always thought he did. When we got together, he lived in a very posh neighborhood. At least, that's what he told me. I remember I wanted to see his house, and it was being painted. There was always some reason that I never got to see his home. The bastard used me."

"How long have you been together?"

"A year. I was so happy with Richard. I would never have known he didn't have money. We were always going places. Now that I think about it, I paid for everything. He sold his business, so he was in between jobs. I'm sure all of that was a lie."

"Our buddy is checking him out. They'll call when they hear something."

"Jeez, I almost dread hearing what they say. I've been a complete idiot. I thought he loved me…" He started crying, and he wouldn't stop. "I was a fool. He must have thought I was Mr. Gullible."

I threw him some napkins from the glove compartment. *Taco bell always gives me more napkins than I can use. Those extra napkins come in handy.*

"Thank you, Grayson, for the napkins."

"You're welcome. Thomas, you might be happy that you found out how Richard was before he spent your money."

"That reminds me, I need to stop my credit cards and get him off my bank accounts. I'm just glad we didn't get married. We were going to tie the knot in June. Richard wanted us to get married six months ago. I'm so happy I listened to Myrtle. She told me to wait a year before getting married. That stinking bastard; I'll ruin him. He won't be able to show his face."

We pulled into Florence around three in the morning. All three of us were ready to drop. I put the groceries away and then found my bed.

"The following day, I gave Thomas my phone, and he called his bank to make sure Richard couldn't use anything. Then he called his credit card companies and did the same. Then we all went fishing. The house sat on the river, and it was beautiful. We fished until we had enough for dinner. I grilled fish, and Thomas made fries. I felt bad for Thomas, but he was lucky he discovered what was happening now rather than later. We were there two days before Ryker called and told us about Richard.

I looked at Thomas as Ryker read off all the illegal stuff Richard was involved in. When I hung up, I told Thomas everything. "First of all, Richard is married. He has three kids, and his wife hasn't seen him in two years. She lives in Crescent City with her sister's family. He beat her pretty severely before he left. He took their only car and cleaned out the bank account. There is a warrant out for his arrest."

"Oh my God, I was so blind, that poor woman. Wow, so he was married to a woman."

"Do you think he's gay, or did he pretend to be gay? He may have planned on killing you after your marriage which wouldn't have been real. But he would have had all of your things by then."

"I'm sure that's what he planned on doing. He kept asking me to put him in my will. I almost did it. I believe he really was gay. He knew more than I did about our kind of sex."

"I say you were lucky he put that GPS on our vehicle."

"I agree with you. I'm sure Richard would have killed me after we married. Wow, do I have a story for Myrtle. I'm surprised he kept his real name."

"Yeah, he wasn't thinking clearly."

"Oh yeah, we get to go home. They sent the Iranian back to Iran."

"What about his family."

"The daughter is in foster care. The wife wanted to return with him. He won't be allowed back in the United States."

"I would love to foster Gina. She and I were good friends."

"We'll help you talk to the foster care people."

17

GILLY

I waited for Lucy to pick up the girls. I began to get scared when she wouldn't answer her phone. I heard my phone ding and checked my message. There was a picture of Lucy tied up in the back seat of a truck. A white truck. The message said, 'If I can't have you, then I'll take Lucy.' I quickly called the police. I wanted to scream, but I had the girls. I couldn't even cry. I then called Adam. I knew he would find Lucy.

"Hello."

"Adam, I'm so scared. I'm sending you a screenshot I just received. I know it's that fucking Ron. He has Lucy. The police are on their way. I don't know what to do."

"Fuck."

The phone went dead.

I called the Seals. I talked to Hutch, who said he would be right over. I sent him a screenshot, also. I was pacing back and forth when the police walked into the shop. I told them not to scare the girls. Then I called to see if Betty could come over and take the girls up to my apartment.

"I'll be right there. We'll catch this guy. Don't you worry, honey The Seals will get Lucy back."

After telling the police about Ron, I showed them the screenshot. "We need to take your phone for evidence."

"No, I need this phone. It's the only link I have. Nope, I'll send the screenshot to your phone. If I get more, I'll send you everything I get. You have to get this guy. He's horrible. He'll hurt her bad. He might kill her." *Calm down, Gilly. You'll scare the kids.*

Hutch walked inside and hugged me. He looked over at the kids. "Your aunt is coming over to help with the children.

"Hutch, this guy is crazy. You have to find her."

"Do you know him?"

"Yes." I took his hand and pulled him where the kids couldn't hear. "He is a monster. It started in high school. He raped me so many times. He beat me, and he would bite me. He never did it where anyone could see. He always said he would kill Lucy if I told anyone. I was so frightened all the time."

"When I left for college, I would only visit on holidays. This last time I went home, he tried raping me on the beach. I got away. Adam beat him and told him to leave me alone or he would kill him. The police in my hometown know about him. He should have been locked up a long time ago. I was so scared to say anything at that time."

"Who is Adam?"

"He's Lucy's ex-husband. I already called him. He'll be here soon. But we have to find her. This guy enjoys causing pain. He'll hurt her as much as he can to see the pain he is causing or get back at me."

"We'll find them. Our town is small. There aren't too

many places he can hide. We'll wait for another call from him."

I fixed the kids something to eat and then made all of us a cup of coffee. Then I waited for my phone to ring.

I raised my head when the shop door opened two hours later, and Adam walked in. I ran to him. "What are we going to do?"

He looked around, and Layla ran to him. "I missed you, Daddy."

"I missed you too, sweetheart."

Then three-year-old Maddie ran to him. He picked her up and held her. He kissed her nose. "I missed you too, Maddie."

"Dada." He saw Gracie sitting in her playpen, picked her up, and kissed her. I was surprised he knew them and that they knew him. *Why do Gracie and Maddie call Adam Dada? He must be with them more than I thought.*

Betty came in and took the kids upstairs to my apartment. I introduced Adam and Hutch, but they shook hands as if they knew each other. "Do you two know each other?"

"Yes, Adam has been working with some friends of ours. We've been involved in the same case that he has been working on for years."

"Doing what."

"A little undercover work."

"Tell me everything that is going on here," Adam demanded, changing the subject.

I told him everything. Then my phone rang.

"Hello."

"Don't do a fucking thing, he says," Lucy shouted into the phone. Then she screamed, in pain.

Adam grabbed the phone from my hand. "I'm going to kill you this time, you bastard!" Adam shouted. "You touched what is mine." The phone went dead. "I knew I should have killed him."

I was crying, I heard Lucy call Adam's name before the phone shut off. "Where is she?"

"They're near the water," Adam said. "I could hear the waves."

I paced as Hutch called people. My door opened, and I turned as Gray and Gabe walked in. He pulled me into his arms. "Grayson, he's here, and he has Lucy."

"I know, sweetheart. We'll find them."

I showed him the text I shared with everyone. "He's beaten her. We have to find Lucy before he kills her."

He kept his arm around me as he walked to where Adam stood. He shook his hand. "Long time no see. What have you been doing?"

"The same thing I was doing the last time we talked."

"Maybe, he's the wrong guy."

"No, he's not. I feel it in my gut."

"Who are you talking about?" No one answered me. I wondered what they were trying to keep secret.

"I recognize these rocks. He took Lucy to the lighthouse. We need to plan before we rush there. We can't drive a car. He'll see the headlights miles away. We'll go in from the water. He won't even think about watching the sea. Let's go. Sweetheart, you wait here. We'll call you when we have Lucy."

"Are you serious? I'm going with you. My sister needs me."

"You won't be any good to her dead. Stay here."

I saw the look Adam gave Gray like he must be crazy.

"Look, Gillian, sweetheart. You have to listen to me. I don't have time to argue. Please stay here. I can't worry about you getting in our way."

"You look, Grayson! I won't get in anyone's way. I can either go with you guys or go on my own."

"Let's go. Gilly's coming with us," Adam said, walking out the door.

"How do you know, Adam?" Gray asked.

"He's Lucy's ex-husband." I followed Adam outside, and the others followed us.

"Fuck," Gray said behind me. "You stay by my side. Whatever I tell you to do, you do it." He took my hand, pulled me into his arms, and kissed me. I wrapped my arms around him.

"I'm glad you're back. Even if you are bossy."

"We'll get her. But I don't want your life to be in danger."

"I know. But I also know how this guy's brain works. He thinks he controls me even after all this time. I should have turned him in when we were in high school. But I was scared." I closed my mouth, and we didn't say another word.

When we were close enough where he might see our headlights, Hutch turned the lights out. We drove as close as we dared. He opened the back of the vehicle, and there were wet suits. Everyone grabbed one and put them on, while I waited on the other side.

I had decided to make my way to the lighthouse on foot. I wouldn't bring attention to myself, but I would be there if something happened and Lucy needed me. I was almost there when I heard her scream. I ran the rest of the way. I saw three wet suits climbing up the lighthouse steps. I couldn't determine who they were. Then I saw two running up the steps. I started praying that Lucy was there.

"Fuck!" I heard Adam scream.

My phone binged. I read the message: 'You guys are falling into my trap. Why do you think I let the lighthouse get into my photo? This is so much fun. Another picture is on its way.'

I heard a bing and screamed until Gray and Adam reached me. I handed the phone to Adam. He roared so loud, I cried out again. "Is she dead?"

Grayson looked at the photo. He made it larger. "No, she is alive."

"How can you tell?"

"One of her eyes is peeking at the camera."

Adam roared again. Then he looked at me. "I forced her to move. I purposely made it horrible for her to live there. I was trying to catch my fucking father. We believe he's working with the cartel in China. For five years, I've been trying to catch that bastard. He is fucking scum. I didn't want Lucy and Layla anywhere around him. I didn't fight for her. Now it's too late."

"No, it's not. Didn't you hear Gray? He said Lucy was alive." I showed him what Gray showed me. He sat down and ran his hands through his hair. "Where do you think she is?" I asked Gray.

Gray paced back and forth. "I think they might be at her place. There are only a few places to hide around here, especially with him knowing the police will be hunting for him. We'll keep these on because they are black. If you come with us, and they are there, you have to stay in the vehicle until we catch him. This is not something up for debate."

I nodded my head, and we climbed back into the vehicle. "We have to find them. I know how crazy Ron is. He won't think anything about killing Lucy. We have to save her."

"We will, sweetheart."

We spotted the white truck hiding in the alley. "There is a side door, it might be locked, but it goes into the laundry room. I'm sure he's made sure everything is locked up. His mom was a realtor, so he could get into vacant homes. The first thing he did was lock everything, even the windows."

"Gilly, you have to keep the doors locked until we get back. I want you to stay in the vehicle. Do not get out. Okay."

I stayed behind as they walked toward Lucy's home. I didn't know what to do. I got out of the vehicle and leaned against it, waiting. That's when I heard Gray shout my name. Before I could take off running, I was grabbed from behind and dragged down the alley. I was slugged in the face until I blacked out.

Has anyone ever beaten you and thrown you in the back of his car. It was so frigging scary. I knew I was in the car's trunk when I woke up. I felt for the tail lights. I knew what I had to do. I had to knock a tail light out and stick my hands out so people could see I was in the car's trunk. I couldn't find it. Finally, I felt it and slammed it repeatedly with my hands. I knew my hands were bleeding, but I didn't stop. I had to remove all of this hard plastic to stick my hand out.

My face was hurting from him slugging me. It felt like it was swollen. My lips hurt. I tried licking them, but that made it hurt worse. I felt around in the trunk for something hard to hit against the plastic. I felt something. I reached for it and prayed.

Yes, it's a screwdriver. I cried because I knew this would work. I beat the screwdriver against the hard plastic and still couldn't get my hand out. I hit it some more until, finally, I could get my hand through it. I waved my hand around and around, hoping someone saw me. And all the time I prayed he hadn't killed my sister.

What is he doing? I felt the car slow down as he pulled over. I readied to kick him hard when he opened the trunk.

When the trunk opened, he laughed. The sound was so scary I felt pure fear.

Then I kicked him right in the face. He grabbed my leg and punched me. We were fighting each other when a car pulled up next to us. I heard a woman shout for him to stop. "Go, he'll kill you!" I screamed at her. "Hurry! Leave!" I cried as I heard her leaving. I knew she would call the cops. But we would be long gone. He zip-tied my hands and slammed the trunk down.

I can't do anything to help myself. But I will save myself. How am I going to save myself? I can't let him kill me. Lucy, please don't be dead. I'm so sorry I brought this monster around you and the kids.

I allowed myself a moment to cry. I deserved that moment. Now, enough was enough.

I had to kill this bastard. *How will I do that? Where is the screwdriver?* I wiggled around to see if I could feel it anywhere. I felt it up by my head.

Then I heard the sirens. I could see the flashing lights through the broken tail light. He'd never get away from the police. I felt him pulling over. I'd scream when I hear them get out of their car. I listened as the police opened their car door. "Help me! Please help me!" I heard the gunshots, and then the car peeled out, and we were racing down the road. *Oh my God, he shot the policeman.*

18

GRAY

We had to find her. I saw the lights flashing and pulled over. I jumped out of the vehicle and ran to where a woman was with the shot officer. "What happened?"

"That guy shot him. I have an ambulance coming. You have to help that woman. She's in the trunk of his car. She broke the tail light out. It's a dark Grand Prix. He's going to kill her. This policeman pulled him over. Hurry before he kills her."

My heart was beating so hard. I couldn't believe he'd gotten this far. "Fuck! I can't believe this is happening. I'm going to kill him with my bare hands."

Hutch looked at me. "We have to keep a clear head. He's not that far up ahead. We'll catch them, but we don't want to lose it. Calm down. I saw the car in the ditch. It had to be the same one: a dark Grand Prix. I was out of the car before it stopped.

I saw the trunk up, and no one was in it. I held up my hand for Hutch to stop walking and listened. I heard her scream. I ran as fast as my legs would take me. Hutch ran beside me. We saw them ahead, and a bullet whizzed past my head. I kept on running straight for him. "Try hitting a moving target, fucker!" I shouted.

"Gray, be careful. He's crazy," Gilly screamed. Then I heard another shot go off and crazy laughter.

"Call me crazy now, bitch. What's the matter? Does the bullet have your tongue?"

I roared loud enough for everyone to hear. I took my gun out and shot him in the head. He fell to the ground dead. I dropped to my knees beside Gilly. "Sweetheart, please say something. Gilly, darling." I couldn't see where she was shot. I picked her up and headed to my vehicle.

The police pulled up at the same time as an ambulance. I ran with Gilly. Hutch went to the police. I carried her to the back of the ambulance. She was beaten, her face was swollen, and her hands were cut up. I cut the zip tie from her wrist. Her hands were bloodied and cut. I was sure it was from trying to get the tail light out. I let the EMT work on her. When he struggled to get her top off, he cut it off with scissors. I could see he was nervous.

"Is this your first day on the job?" I demanded.

"No, sir, it's my second."

"Get out of there." He jumped out, and I jumped in. I saw where the bullet went in. It didn't look good. The other EMT worker was on the phone with a doctor. When Gilly stopped breathing, I started giving her CPR right away. I worked for a few minutes before she took a breath. Gilly opened her eyes as much as she could. Her eyes were swollen shut. They were glazed over, but I knew she could see me.

"Hey, sweetheart." We were flying down the road to the hospital. "Don't try and talk." Her lips were all split.

"Gray, I'm sorry. I want to tell you goodbye. I never told you this, but I love you."

"I love you too, sweetheart—you're not telling me goodbye. You're going to be okay. I know you will be." I bent my head and kissed her. Then the EMT started working on her. I wasn't able to keep the woman I love safe. I should have kept her with me. I should have known she wouldn't stay in the vehicle. We pulled up to the emergency room, and Adam was there.

He looked at Gilly, "What the fuck happened to her?"

"He beat her, and then he shot her. We ran inside the ER behind her stretcher. They tried blocking us. We pushed them out of the way.

"Where is Lucy?"

"She's here. They put her to sleep. She was so upset about Gilly that they feared she would hurt herself. I'll take her home when she wakes up. How's Gilly?"

"He shot her in the back. Hopefully, it didn't hit anything. I shot that fucker between the eyes. Why the hell are you still working on that case?"

"Because my dad hasn't let me in on anything, it's almost like he knows I'm waiting for that moment when they haul his ass to prison. My father is running the business for the cartel. I know he is. I know he killed my mom, and he will pay, but I need proof. I've caused so much pain to Lucy and my family. I had to get Lucy out of that house. My dad doesn't like Lucy. He hasn't killed her because I told him if he touched her, I would kill him."

"Do you still love her?"

"I'll always love her. She kept trying to make me claim her. It was hard not to tell her what I was doing, but I couldn't do that. My father would kill Lucy and the kids."

"What are you going to do?"

"I'll stay here for a week to help Lucy. I can't stay any longer without my father working something up in his evil brain."

"I'm sorry you have that bastard for a father."

"Yeah, me too."

I looked up when someone walked down the hallway, almost running. It was a woman and a man. I could tell the woman had been crying.

"Alice," Adam said, hugging her. "John, I thought the police were going to keep an eye on that bastard."

"Is he locked up?"

"No, he's dead."

"Good, I hope he rots in hell. Where are my daughters?"

"Alice, this is Gray."

"Gray, so you are my daughter's wrong date. Where were you when this was going on?"

"I was out of town. I got back in time to save Gilly, but I couldn't. I'm sorry."

Alice shook her head and waved my words away. "I know you told Gilly to stay in the vehicle with locked doors."

"Gilly never was good at listening to advice. How is she?"

"She's in surgery. He shot her in the back and she was beaten badly. We can only pray she pulls through the surgery."

"Adam, will you take me to Lucy?"

"Yes, she's sleeping because they had to give her a shot. The girls are at Gilly's with a woman named Betty."

"Betty is my aunt. The kids are safe with her."

"Will you tell her I said thank you for watching the children? As soon as Gilly is out of surgery and I know she's alright, I'll get the kids."

"Don't worry about any of that right now. The kids are okay, and my aunt doesn't mind keeping them."

She nodded and wiped her eyes. She had emerald green eyes like Gilly. There wasn't one spot in that hospital I didn't walk. I talked to all the nurses; they all knew Lucy because she was a nurse at the hospital.

I knew they were having Lucy stay another night, and that's when I realized it was morning. Gilly had been in surgery for seven hours. I made my way to Lucy's room. Adam was sitting in a chair by the window, and Alice was asleep on a small reclining chair. I knew John had gone to Lucy's home to clean up the mess that was made there.

"Have you heard anything?"

I looked at Adam and shook my head. Before I finished speaking, Griffin Madden walked into the room. He was a spinal specialist. I looked at him frowning, "How come you are here? Did they call you to look at Gilly?"

"Yes, she's out of surgery. The bullet was close to her spine, I got all of it out. Now we have to wait and see when she will wake up. I'm assuming he beat her in the head with the butt of the gun. Her head is swollen, and we might have to let the pressure off her brain. She'll be in intensive care by now if someone wants to visit her—two people at a time."

"Thank you, Griff."

Alice was sitting up now. "Alice, would you like to go with me?"

"Yes."

We walked quietly to the ICU unit. I picked up the phone and told them we were there to visit Gilly. They opened the doors, and we walked inside. A nurse was waiting for us. She showed us where Gilly was. I was glad I had a hold of Alice because her legs gave out when she saw her daughter lying in that bed. You couldn't tell it was even Gilly. Her head was so swollen you couldn't see her eyes or anything that would tell you the person in the bed was Gilly

Marshall. Her long, beautiful, dark hair was matted and covered in mud and blood.

"I can't believe this is my daughter, Gilly," Alice said, picking one of her hands up. They were covered in cuts and bruises. There was not a spot on her that wasn't bruised and beaten. I watched Alice kiss her fingers and her forehead. She said a prayer for Gilly to heal quickly. Then she looked at me, "I'm going back to Lucy's room. Will you please come and get me when Gilly wakes up?"

"Of course I will. Do you want me to walk with you?"

"No, I'm going to stop and get Adam and me some coffee."

I sat down in the chair and touched Gilly's fingers. There were so many machines making so much noise. I felt someone stand next to me, and I looked over. It was Griff.

"It looks way worse than it is. We have everything hooked up to her to keep an eye on her. We can see how her brain waves are functioning. The most important thing is that she is breathing on her own. She's going to be sleeping for hours still. Why don't you go home and shower? You are covered in dried blood?"

I looked down at myself. I remembered I hadn't been home since we got back from our job. "I have clean clothes in my vehicle. Can I shower here somewhere?"

"Come with me, and I'll show you where you can. If you get caught, don't tell them I said you can use the shower. Most of the people who work here don't like me."

"I can't believe that. Doctor Griffin Madden; everyone loves you."

"Yeah, right. I have another patient to check on. I'll see you later."

"Griff, thank you for being here."

"You're welcome."\

19

GRAY

I looked at Gilly, and she was still sleeping three days later. I thought she might be waking up. Her eyes were starting to move around. Her swelling went down on its own, so they didn't have to take pressure off her brain. Her mom walked in and handed me a sandwich and a soda.

"You should go home and get some rest."

I looked over at the door, and Lucy walked into the room, the three little ones with her.

"Hey, sweetheart," Alice said, hugging her. Then she picked up the baby. "Why are you out here on your own, with these babies? You look so much better. How do you feel."

"Mom, I feel good. I only hurt a little now. I'm fine. How is Gilly?"

I got up and went over and hugged Lucy. "I see movement in her eyes. That's a good sign. Griff said the swelling going down was super good news. I think she looks so much better."

"Gray, you're right. She does look better. I think she'll be waking up any time now. have you gone home yet?"

"I'm afraid she'll wake up, and I won't be here. She told me she loved me, and I told her I loved her too. I wish she would wake up. Is Adam around?"

"He's leaving today."

Was that a catch in her voice? I knew why they weren't together. It was because Adam didn't want her around his fucking father. *He needs help with this. It's been going on for five frigging years. I'll talk to Mace. We'll join his motorcycle gang. We should have done this initially, but I honestly thought it was finished. Why has the DEA let this go on for so long? I will call Lucas, and Ryan and see if he can find anything out. Why should two people who love each other not be together? Sure it is strange. Lucy tried to get him to admit he loved her by getting married twice. Different strokes for different folks, I guess.*

"Can you please call me when Gilly wakes up?"

"You'll be the first person I call."

"Thank you. Mom, why don't you and John come for dinner tonight."

"That would be lovely, dear. What time should we be there?"

"Come early so we can visit." As I watched, she started to cry. I pulled her to me and hugged her.

"Everything is going to work out. Before you know it, your life will fall into place—your life and Gilly's."

"I hope so. It's been a long time coming. I'm through crying for now. Thank you for loving my sister. You'll see how lucky you are to have Gilly to love you. She's fiercely protective of those she loves, as she proved by trying to save me when she was in high school."

"We have to move on with our life. I don't believe Gilly would want to remember that time of her life. We have to live for today. Looking in the rearview mirror never works. That man is dead. He'll never hurt anyone again."

"I know. You're right. I will try my hardest never to think of that bastard again."

As soon as they left, I got on the phone. "Hey, Lucas, Ryan, it's Gray Campbell. I talked to Adam Wilson. Why the fuck is he still trying to catch his father? I'm sending Mace and a couple of others there. They can pretend to be in a motorcycle gang."

"Damn, I thought that was finished. Why didn't he call someone? I'll see if I can get some people here to join the same gang."

"Good, the sooner, the better. Let me tell you something. That bastard is crazy. Adam believes he killed his mother. That's why he wants to see this through to the end. We need to speed this up and make the end sooner rather than later before it destroys Adam and the ones he loves."

"I'll take care of it. Don't send Mace or anyone else. Thanks for calling, Gray."

"I'll talk to you later, Hutch."

I put my phone away and turned to the bed. Gilly watched me with a smile on her face. I dropped to my knees next to the bed. I softly kissed her lips. "Hey, I love you." She smiled, closed her eyes again, and went back to sleep. I called for a nurse. Then I called Lucy and Alice. Both of them cried over the phone.

"She went back to sleep, but she woke up. That's what matters."

"Yes, this is the best news you could give me."

∽

I LOOKED AT GRIFFIN, shaking my head. I was tired of arguing with these people. "I told you, and I will tell you again: She woke up. I told her I loved her, and she smiled at me."

"I believe you, Gray. But that doesn't mean her brain woke up with her. She smiled at you because that was a reflex. You heard what the specialist said. Gilly was beaten. The back of her head was hit so many times. It's like each hit is an injury that has to heal. The main thing is that the swelling has gone down, giving her head a chance to recover from each blow to her skull. She will wake up completely. It'll take a few more days. We have to all have patience."

Lucy had gone back to work. She walked over and kissed Gilly and hugged me. "I have to get back to my floor. I'll check on her when I have a break."

"I'll see you later."

I stretched my arms over my head and bent at my waist. Then I started doing push-ups.

"Gray..." I jumped up and hurried to the bed, almost tripping over my own two feet. "What are you doing?" Her voice was scratchy sounding. I hit the nurse button.

"I was doing push-ups. How do you feel, sweetheart?"

"Drowsy. How long have I been sleeping?"

"Almost three weeks."

"What? How is Lucy?"

"Lucy is fine," she said, walking into the room. "Let me raise you and give you a small drink of water."

"Lucy, I'm sorry I brought that monster to your house." Her voice was so scratchy I felt the pain in it. She took a sip of water.

"Shhh, the bastard is dead. Gray killed him. We don't have to worry about him anymore."

"I'm so glad he's dead. She turned and looked at me and smiled. Thank you for killing him."

"Sweetheart, I will kill anyone who hurts you."

"I'm sorry I didn't stay inside the vehicle."

"I only want you to get better. I love you."

"I heard you telling me you loved me when I was sleeping. I love you too." She closed her eyes and went back to sleep.

Lucy looked at me, smiling. "She's going to be okay. I'll call her doctor and let him know what is going on. She's going to be okay." She hugged me again and a tear fell down her cheek. "Thank you for loving my sister."

"Why are you crying?" Alice asked, walking into the room.

"Because my sister will be okay. She talked to Gray and me."

"My prayers have been answered. I'm so happy. Did you call and let Adam know Gilly's going to be okay?"

"Mom, it just now happened. No, I haven't called Adam. Why don't you call him for me?"

"Okay, I'll do that."

20

GILLY

It's been a month since I woke up. *Why can't my body move normally? Griffin said it would take time. I'm doing therapy. I'm doing all the exercises I'm supposed to be doing, but nothing is working. I limp when I walk. Why is that? I looked up as someone walked into my coffee shop.*

"Ryker, how have you been?"

"I've been good. How are you doing?"

"I'm good, except for the limp. The doctors don't understand why I limp."

Ryker ran his hand through his hair and smiled with his dimple showing. "I don't know if this will help, but I met this man once. He had been shot in the hip and told me he had a limp for a long time until he joined the woman's yoga class. He said they had him stretching his body in all different directions. He said his muscles were bunched up. Even though he was in therapy and exercising, they weren't working as the yoga did. You might want to try a little yoga."

"You are a genius. Of course, that's what it is."

"I'm not saying that's the problem, but what can it hurt

to try? If it hurts when you stretch, your muscles may need stretching."

"I'll join a yoga class today. It gives me something to look forward to." I handed his coffee to him and said goodbye. Thirty minutes later, I joined a yoga class. When Lucy and the kids walked in, I was smiling.

"Why are you so happy?"

"I've signed up for a yoga class. Ryker suggested that I take a yoga class to stretch my muscles. Don't you think that's a great idea?"

"Yes, I think it is."

"You should join me. The first class is tonight."

"I might join later. I'm not feeling that good right now."

"Are you sick?"

"No, I'm just a little run down. I'm taking a vacation. Even though I was off work for a while, I needed more time. I'm going to take the kids to the park today. We want some hot chocolate and donuts. We are having a picnic. It's so beautiful here. The best thing I could have done was to move to this beautiful small town. Thank you for talking me into it."

"I'm glad you decided to move here. I hope you have a nice picnic. This is a perfect day for one."

"Yes, it is. I wish you could go with us."

"Me too, but there is no one to work at the shop."

"We will see you later. Goodbye, Gilly."

"Bye."

I owed Betty so much for keeping my shop open. I looked around and sighed. I loved having this little shop. Sometimes I wanted to do something else, but that was because I'd done engineering for eight years. I didn't want to be an engineer on oil rigs, but sometimes my mind said it wanted to do more. But I ignored those thoughts. I was staying right here in beautiful Cedar Falls. I wasn't moving away. I walked out and sat at one of the cute tables I had put out front. I drank my coffee and watched the people walk by.

I saw a dark car slow down as it drove by and had a creepy feeling. I knew it was because of what happened to me. I tried not to think of that. I was glad Gray killed that bastard. When the black vehicle parked at the end of the street and no one got out, I went back inside.

It was so quiet, I turned some music on, and then I couldn't stop myself. I stepped back outside and looked where the car was parked. It was gone. I smiled and shook my head—just like me to get all wacko over a black vehicle even though it did have really dark windows.

I wanted to pull my hair out by closing time, not that it wasn't busy. I always had lots of customers. My problem is that I'm used to working out issues on the computer. I've always used my mind. *But I came here to change my life. I wanted to slow my life down and do something else. That is what I'm doing.* I was okay with my job and my shop before getting attacked. I'm still okay with it. I dressed in my leggings and went to my yoga class.

The class had about twenty women, even a couple of guys. I signed up for the beginner class. I had those moves down in no time.

"You're doing great, Gilly. Are you sure you've never done this before?"

I chuckled. "I'm sure. I used to run ten miles every morning. That's about all the stretching I gave to my muscles. I'm hoping this helps me to stop limping."

"Tell me about your limping."

"I was in an accident, and I started limping."

"We know about your accident. I'm sorry you had to go through that horrible experience."

"Thanks. I want to forget the entire thing."

"I don't blame you. I have another class that is one step up from this one if you want to join it instead."

"No, I think I'll work my way up." What I really thought was that I would buy a video, and Lucy and I could do yoga together. This woman hadn't left my side since we started the class. I wondered why she didn't attend to the other people in the group. I wished she would move away. She wanted all the details about what had happened to me. I decided to concentrate on my stretching until she finally moved away.

As soon as I got home, I called Lucy and told her I would get us a video and do yoga together. "The instructor was really intrusive. She started talking about my accident. I know she wanted me to tell her every detail."

"I had a strange thing happen when I was at the park. A black car drove by and took pictures of the kids and me. I wonder why they would do that?"

"You know something, Lucy, do you mind if I stay with you tonight? I feel kind of jittery. I'm sure it's because of the instructor."

"Grab your pajamas and get over here. I would also like the company."

"Lucy and I stayed up and talked as we ate popcorn and drank Pepsi. It was like when we were teenagers when we still lived at home."

I had my alarm set for five-thirty and climbed out of bed. I went to the kitchen and put a pot of coffee on when Lucy walked in. "Are you off today? Never mind, I remember you are on vacation. How about a cup of coffee?" Instead of answering, she made a mad dash for the bathroom. I ran after her. "Are you sick?"

"Only in the mornings."

"What do you mean."

"I'm pregnant."

I grabbed the counter and almost fainted. "That fucker raped you."

"No, sweetie, hell no! I'm not having his baby."

"Then who's baby are you having?"

She looked at me like she wanted to pull her hair out and scream. "I'm pregnant with Adam's child. We can't tell him. I don't want him to know. I asked him to make love to me. But that doesn't mean we will be together. He is still in that toxic place with his dad and all those bikers. He chose them over me. That part hasn't changed. I think his dad is in a bunch of other things. He's a horrible bastard. I hate him. The moment I met him, I knew he was trouble. At least Adam broke it off with his fiancé."

That's when I remembered Adam being there when Lucy was missing. I remember he knew Gray and some of the others. I remembered him roaring in anger and helplessness. Because that monster took the woman he loved, it was coming back. He said his dad was trafficking kids, and he was trying to catch him. He was working with the DEA. I decided not to say anything to Lucy. Later, if I had to tell her, I would.

"I won't say a word. Don't let the kids know. Layla is the one who likes to share news about new babies."

"Layla likes to share news about everything. So if you don't want every person to know your entire life, don't say anything when her little ears can hear you."

"We are happy about the baby, right?"

Lucy shut the bathroom door as tears fell onto her cheeks. I had tears falling from my eyes.

"I am so happy about this baby. I know that's crazy. I already have three daughters and no husband. I know this baby is a boy. I want this baby. When Adam was with me that night, I prayed we would make his son."

"I knew it was all we would have. I knew I was pregnant three weeks ago. I didn't say anything because I know how crazy it is that I keep having kids. Can we please not tell anyone, not even mom? She would call Adam and tell him. She tells him everything."

"I won't tell a soul. We'll say you're getting fat when you start gaining weight." We sat on the bathroom floor and laughed and cried. "I have to leave. You know the coffee shop has to be opened."

"I know you have to go. Why don't we do something on your day off tomorrow."

"I would love that. Let's be thinking of something to do. Lock your doors when I leave."

"Always. Why don't you leave your pajamas here, and you can stay with me. I'll cook us dinner."

"Perfect. Thank you, Lucy, for letting me spend the night and not asking why."

"I'm glad you came over. I was a little nervous after that guy took our picture."

"Yeah, that was strange." I didn't mention seeing the black car. That gave me the creeps. Was someone following us? Maybe I should call Adam and see if he has someone following us.

21

GRAY

I was ready to leave. It'd been three weeks, and I wanted to go home. I wanted to see for myself that Gilly was alright. I wanted to hold her in my arms all night long. God, I loved that woman. I planned on asking her to marry me when I got home. I looked at Gabe. "Who do you talk to when discussing your life?"

"No one. I never discuss my life with anyone. If I worry, I talk to myself."

"Why don't you talk to one of your brothers?"

Gabe looked at me like I was a crazy person. "Are you kidding me? Do you talk to your brother, Hutch, about your problems? I'm sure the answer is no. Which brother would I talk to? Jack, he'd hit me up the side of the head. Dan would laugh if I asked to speak with him; and Jake would call my parents and tell them something was wrong with me. No, I figure it all out myself. Why do you need to talk to me about something?"

"I'm thinking about asking Gilly to marry me."

"Why would you do that? That would scare her off. Gilly hasn't even gotten her life settled. She isn't going to keep the shop. She might keep it, but she'll hire others to run it. I could see the restlessness in her eyes. I mean, she's an engineer. She's used to excitement in her job. She worked in exciting and dangerous places. She has a lot of shit going on right now. Do you think it's a good time to ask her to marry you?"

"Yes, I do. I think any time for us is the right time. Gilly loves living in Cedar Falls, but more importantly, she loves me. She's not going to pack up and move away."

"I didn't say she was going to move away. I said she would look for another job soon to keep her mind busy."

"Okay, I agree she will have to find something to keep busy. But she loves me. She won't move away. Plus, Lucy lives in Cedar Falls. I want Gilly as my wife."

"Maybe we can put our heads together and see what exciting things she can do in our town."

I heard Gabe chuckle. "To be honest, I've been worried about that myself. I have to find her something to do. Have you any ideas?"

"Why don't we try and set something up for her that will keep her mind busy? What does she like doing?"

"I did hear that Joe Peterson was selling his shipyard business. Everything goes with it. All those broken-down boats. That would keep her happy for years."

"Why do you think she likes working on old boats? Do you feel that she might leave town?"

"No, I feel like she might try and find work that will take her away most of the time. I'll mention it to her when I see her." I nodded, glad I decided to find something to keep her busy. I looked around. We were almost home. I was excited to see Gilly. I always wanted her with me. I would wait a month before I asked her to marry me.

"What do you mean, she left to do a job for Gerald? Does she plan on coming back here?"

"Yes, don't worry. Gilly will be back here in no time. She was getting a little bored, so when Gerald called her, she agreed to do this one job. She left you a letter. Let me get it," Lucy said.

"Why didn't she just call and tell me herself?"

"She tried, but your voicemail is full."

"Oh, okay. Thank you. I'm sorry if I was snappy. It's just that I've missed Gilly so much."

"I know. She missed you too."

"How is she?"

"She's good. She'll be back before you know it. Would you like a cup of tea?"

"No, thank you. I need to pick up my puppy today."

"You're getting a puppy. Yes, my friend Noah, and his wife, Sofie, have ten puppies. Their dog got loose for two days, and they noticed she was gaining weight when she got home. Sofie took her to the vet, and she was pregnant. Would you like a puppy?"

"Oh, that would be wonderful. Can we please go with you and get it today? I'll have to get some dog food. This is so exciting. The girls are going to love having a puppy. I'll have to potty train it. Why don't we take my vehicle? Then we won't have to take the car seats out. You can drive... Girls, I have something exciting to tell you," she said, leaving the room.

My mind wasn't on Lucy and the puppies. My mind was on Gerald and Gilly. What was he trying to do? Did he hope to win Gilly back?

"You don't have to worry about Gilly and Gerald. Gilly loves you. She would never be with Gerald."

"Was I talking out loud?"

"No, but I saw the worried look when I told you where she was. Can you carry Gracie? I'll get the diaper bag. One thing about having kids is that you are always toting around a large bag full of their needs. Believe me, if you leave anything behind, they will tell you about it. In a loud little voice. Here are my keys."

I chuckled as I buckled the baby into her car seat. She smiled at me. "I think Gracie is getting a tooth on the top."

"Yes, she is. So I have to ensure I have her teething ring for her to chew on." She giggled, "That sounds like she's a puppy. I'll have to get our puppy some chew things. Have you gotten anything for your puppy yet?"

"No, how about we stop at the pet store?"

"That would be great. It's hard doing things alone with three small kids."

"How long have you and Adam been divorced?"

"Almost five years. Just because you divorce someone doesn't mean you stop loving them. I will always love Adam and only Adam. I divorced him because I hated being around his father. He's a horrible man. I don't understand why Adam hasn't kicked him to the curb."

"What about the other two men you married?"

"I never loved them. I know it isn't nice of me to marry someone I don't love. It's just crazy, but I wanted Adam to do something. Like take me away and tell me he loves me. I hate to admit it, but I hoped Adam would come to my wedding and ride off with me on his motorcycle. He never did that. So that's how stupid I was. I went to his house once and saw his father with a little girl. Adam wasn't home, so I left. That has always bothered me. He told me that she was his girlfriend's daughter. I took a photo of them before I left."

I looked over at her as my heart started pounding in my chest. Is this what they needed to catch that bastard? "Where was Adam?"

"I don't know."

I pulled into the Petsmart and carried Gracie inside so Lucy could hold onto the other girl's hand. It took us almost an hour to get everything Lucy and Layla wanted. I only got a few things. I don't know how Lucy could do anything with three little girls. I couldn't wait until I had a chance to call Adam and tell him about the picture Lucy had of his father and the little girl.

22

GILLY

I still didn't understand why Gerald needed me for an emergency. There was no emergency out here on this rig. I was starting to think he wanted me where I was stuck with him alone in the middle of the damn ocean.

"Gerald, why are we here? There is nothing wrong with this rig. I want to go home."

"No, we are going to talk if it takes a month. I'm not calling anyone to pick us up until I find out what is happening with you. Why you broke up with me?"

"Are you kidding me?"

"No, you said you found the guy you fell in love with years ago. But you haven't married him. He would already have that ring on your finger if he loved you."

"Is that why the black car watched me and took photos of Lucy and the kids? "Have you had someone following me?"

"Hell no, I don't do things like that. You know me better than that."

"I do know you better than that. I was hoping you had me followed. A black car was watching me, and they followed Lucy to the park and took photos of her and the girls."

"I can't believe Lucy moved away from Adam. Even after two husbands, she was still in love with him."

"I know, poor Lucy. She loves him so much."

"What about you? Who do you love so much?"

"Grayson Campbell. He's the same guy he was when I first met him."

"I know who he is. He worked for me for years. I never thought he would be someone you would fall for. He's huge. It's like he must work out all the time."

"Gerald, please take me home. I'm not going to change my mind."

"What about how fast you jumped when I called and gave you a chance to inspect this rig? You must be getting bored in Cedar Falls."

"I admit working at the coffee shop is a little slow, but I'll figure something out. I'm not moving. I'm staying where Gray is. I love him."

"You said you loved me?"

"Did I?"

"I wouldn't have asked you to marry me if you didn't love me, would I? Did you tell me you loved me?"

"No, I was never ready to say I love you. That's why I never said I would marry you.

"Do you think you could have married me if you didn't love me?"

"No, I thought I would fall in love with you. You were my dearest friend, I worked so much I didn't know a lot of people, so I didn't have a lot of friends. You were my best friend in San Diego. I knew I loved you, but not the same way you loved me."

" When we first started dating, I told you how I felt when meeting Gray. I never thought I would see him again."

"But there I was on a burning rig, in the middle of the ocean in one of the worst storms ever. He jumped on that burning rig and saved all of us. That isn't why I love him. I love him because my heart knows he is ours. I knew I couldn't let him go. But I didn't go with Gray. I moved to a coastal town in Oregon, and he lived there. If that isn't fate, then what is? I will never love anyone the way I love Grayson. Take me home."

"I'll call the helicopter to pick us up."

We waited for two hours before the helicopter showed up. Gerald wanted me to stay at his place for the night. I refused and took a taxi to the airport. I waited until two in the morning for a plane. When I got home, the sun wasn't even up yet. I walked out on the beach and saw Gray standing there. He must have sensed me there. He turned and walked toward me, and I ran into his arms.

"I missed you, sweetheart."

I raised my face to his. "I missed you too. What are you doing out here?"

"I came out here because my feeling told me you would be home."

"I would have called, but I haven't had a chance to charge my phone. Are you staying with me tonight?"

"Yes, Adam will be here this morning."

"Why?"

"Because I called him. I went over to pick up my puppy, and I took Lucy and the girls with me so they could get one too, she ended up getting two puppies."

"Oh, no, she can't take care of two puppies. I'll go see her tomorrow. What does that have to do with Adam?"

"I was talking to Lucy, and she told me about Adam's

dad. I actually know some things about his dad. But I had reason to be alarmed when she told me she went to see Adam, but he wasn't there. She said his father was with a little girl, and he said the girl was his girlfriend's daughter. She had a feeling about that, so she took pictures. When he turned around, she said the little girl kept looking at her."

"Let's go over there right now. When you were gone, a dark car watched me sit outside, but then Lucy told me a dark car was taking pictures of her and the girls at the park. I asked Adam if he had someone following her. He said no. I stayed at her house for a few nights because we were both shaken."

"We climbed into Gray's vehicle and headed to Lucy's. I was going to wake her up and stay there until Adam showed up.

Her lights were out. We got out of the vehicle and walked up toward the house.

"What the hell are you doing here?"

"I'm coming to make sure my wife is safe."

"Your wife. Lucy hasn't been your wife in years. What if your dad's having you watched?"

"I was careful." He looked at me. "Lucy has always been mine. I let things happen the way they did, so she and the girls would be safe. But she has always been mine."

"Someone took pictures of Lucy and the girls. Your dad needs to be dead. I believe he hates Lucy enough to have her killed."

"You think I don't know that? I would have killed him years ago if I didn't need to know where they were taking those kids. I hate that bastard."

"Why are you guys out here arguing? Who is that? Gilly, what are you doing here?"

"Do you just walk outside when you hear people talking?" Adam demanded.

"Adam, what are you doing here?"

"I'm watching your house. Why didn't you call me and tell me someone took pictures of you and my girls?"

I shook my head. Poor Adam and Lucy. Adam sometimes forgets that two of the girls have different daddies, and Lucy is no longer his wife.

"I thought it was just someone taking pictures of kids playing in the park. Gilly stayed with me for a few nights. Why don't all of you come inside?"

We walked inside and looked at each other. Adam looked at Gray and me. "I thought you were out of town."

"I was. I got home about an hour ago."

"Gilly, you and Gray can leave. Adam is here, so I feel safe enough. Plus, I bought that gun I was telling you I wanted."

"Lucy, I told you not to buy a gun. I said get a mean dog, and you went and bought a gun and got two puppies."

"I think I'll let them out right now."

"Lucy, where is the gun?" Adam asked.

"It's on the fridge."

"No, it's not, Mommy. I have it."

We turned as Layla walked into the kitchen with the gun.

Adam took a step toward his daughter. "Hey, sweetheart, lower your arm." When she lowered it, he walked over and took the gun away. He checked to see if it was loaded. "Don't ever touch another gun. Okay."

"Okay, Daddy."

He picked her up and hugged her. "Now, go back to bed. We'll talk in the morning."

She ran back to her room. "You can leave. I'll be here taking care of my family."

"Adam, we are no longer your family," Lucy said, "God, I can't believe I bought a gun, and my baby had it in her room. What is the matter with me?"

"You were scared. I'm going home. I'll see you later," I said, hugging her.

Lucy hugged me back. She whispered, "Gilly, don't tell anyone about the baby."

I squeezed her to let her know I wouldn't tell anyone. When we were driving back, Gray took a different route. "Where are we going?"

"I wanted to show you something."

We drove on the coastal highway for a few miles until Gray pulled into a place with some old giant boats he pulled into the lot. "What is this place?"

"It's an old shipyard. It's been in the Peterson family for over a hundred years. He's selling it. All of the property goes with it. The dock and everything out here goes with it. It is ours if you like it and want to be my partner in the boat business. I'm leaving it up to you."

I got out of the car and looked around. The sun was shining by now. I walked the property three times, looking at everything. The water was right here. The boat ramp was perfect. I climbed over the broken-down boats. I loved everything about it. It would take a lot of work cleaning the place up. But that was fine with me. This was my stuff, hard work.

I looked at Gray. "I love it. This is it. Are we going to be partners?"

"You probably know more about building boats than I do. But I would love to be your partner."

"Yes," I said as I threw my arms around him. My heart

was beating so fast that I knew what we were doing was something we would have forever, and then our children would have it. I know I was jumping the gun, but I was so excited.

"Let's do it before someone else grabs it."

"I have already bought it. I didn't want to take a chance on losing it."

"I love it. I need to find someone to manage the coffee shop for me. We are going to work great together."

"Sometimes I'll have to go away on a job. But I'll be here as often as I can be."

"I know. Let's go. I'm sleepy. I'll talk to your person and pay my half. I'm going to love working in the shipyard. I wonder if he has any old files I can look at?"

"He gave me everything. It might take you a few years to go through everything. Some papers go back over one hundred years."

"My favorite thing to do is go through old musty papers. You make me happy, Grayson."

"You make me happy, Gilly." I laughed, and he pulled me into him closer. "The first thing we'll do is clean up the office and the other rooms. I want one of those rooms to be a bedroom for when we feel like taking a nap."

I giggled. "Let's hurry. I'm ready to go to bed."

"Me too. Will you tell me about Gerald asking you to inspect a rig?"

"There was nothing wrong with the rig. I finally convinced Gerald I would always love you and only you."

"Good."

23

GRAY

I lay there watching Gilly as she slept. We made love for hours, and now we needed sleep. I closed my eyes and slept. When I opened them again, she was gone. I got up and showered. She gave me one of her drawers. I put on clean clothes and went downstairs.

Gilly smiled when she saw me. She poured me a cup of coffee. I kissed her and pulled her into my arms. "I love you, Gillian Marshall. Will you please marry me so I can wake up with you in my bed every morning?"

"What!"

"I was going to wait to ask you, but I can't wait another minute."

"Yes, I will marry you. Yes! Yes! Yes!"

I picked her up and carried her back upstairs. I was pulling her clothes off when she laughed and grabbed my hands.

"I have to get back downstairs. As much as I want to be with you, I have customers."

I laughed out loud. And we walked back downstairs. "I'm going to see if Hannah wants to manage this shop for me. That way, she can bring the girls here with her. I thought for sure she and Mace would be together by now. I guess neither of them is ready to admit how much they care."

"Everyone has to do their own thing in life. I'm glad Mace is back to his old self. With those girls of his, I knew he would straighten up."

"I'm just glad I found you. It seemed like I was walking around with part of my heart missing."

"You say the hottest things when I can't strip your clothes off. I swear I'm so hard for you. Are you sure we can't lock up for another hour?"

"Hello," Gabe said as he walked inside.

"Hey, Gabe, what would you like to drink."

"A large cup of strong black coffee, please. I'll take an apple fritter too. So, I wonder what the meeting is about this morning."

"We have a meeting this morning? I only slept for a couple of hours. I was hoping to get some more sleep."

"Have you checked your phone messages?"

"No."

"That's okay. I'll tell you what it says. First up, we have a rescue in the Grand Canyon. The flight leaves in an hour. We have a recovery in Alaska, and the plane is waiting on the tarmac. You're going to the Grand Canyon with me. Grab your bag, kiss your girl, we have to go."

"Bye, sweetheart, here are the keys to the boatyard. Be careful climbing on those boats. Hopefully, I'll see you soon."

"Wait, you have to leave. But you just got back. I haven't seen you in almost a month. I want you to stay with me."

"Sweetheart, you know how my job is. At least I'm on land right now and not the sea. I'll call you. I love you."

I watched as she nodded. Tears fell from her eyes. "Baby, I'll be back soon, I promise."

"I know. What is wrong with me? I'm sorry. Of course, you have to go. I'll see you when you get home."

I gave her a lingering kiss. I hated to leave. "I love you."

"I love you too."

I walked down the street to where I parked my truck. I wasn't in a reasonable frame of mind. I didn't want to leave Gilly. I want to regrow the boatyard with her. I still needed to keep working. "I need to run by my house and grab my bag," I said to Gabe as we jumped into my vehicle.

"So, are the two of you going into partnership with the boatyard?"

"Yes, she is all excited. I asked her to marry me, and she said yes. I'm going to take some time off after this trip. Maybe a month and start getting the boatyard cleaned up. That way, all the work won't be on Gilly. Can you believe Gilly's ex-fiancé called her to help with an emergency, and there wasn't an emergency? What an ass."

"Yeah, I heard she went out on a rig. I'm damn glad we no longer go onto that rough sea, I never mentioned this, but that was one job I didn't like at all. How about you?"

"I love the sea. I'm glad to be on dry land now, but I love the ocean. I'm happy I have that in common with Gilly because I plan to go on long sea trips as soon as I can put one of those luxury boats in the yard together."

"I'll be glad to see the shipyard return to its old glory, with shiny new boats instead of the mess there now."

"Me and you both. I wonder how long we'll be gone?"

∼

"Damn, it's hot here. Tell me why I'm riding a mule down a canyon when it's one-hundred and twenty degrees in the shade."

"Someone is defacing and stealing all of the artifacts that have been here forever. They have found two dead bodies that the law here believes are linked together."

I stood on the edge of the Grand Canyon and looked down. The view was spectacular. I took a few pictures and sent them to Gilly. She texted back a selfie of her in the boatyard. I smiled because she was happy. And when Gilly's happy, I'm also happy.

"Where did they find the bodies?" I asked the mayor.

"They found the bodies where the artifacts were stolen." A policeman walked up to them. "They have another body."

"How come you haven't called the FBI or someone like them to investigate this? We're on federal land."

"The people who live here don't trust the government. That's why I called you guys. I was told you could solve this in no time, and that's what we need. I'm not too fond of my tourists getting murdered."

"How were they killed?"

"Snakebite. They must knock the person out and throw the snakes on them."

My insides were shaking, and the one fear I had was snakes—any kind. I didn't want to be around them. Especially the deadly ones."

"Are there a lot of snakes around here?"

"Yes, if you think you hear a rattlesnake, you most likely do, so watch where you step. Here are the mules. You'll have two Indian guides. They know this canyon like the back of their hands."

"Why are we riding mules?" I had never been on a mule

and didn't think I wanted to start right now. First of all, they were slow. We needed to get to that body.

"With the mules, you can look around, and you can go over the body when you come back up. It will be at the morgue. Nothing would be left to a body if we left it down there. The vultures and other animals would have it torn to shreds. This way, you can take photos of anything that looks like it shouldn't be there. Ask your guides anything you want. They're there to help you."

I put my backpack on and got on the mule. I was not too fond of it, but I did it. I looked over at Gabe and laughed. He looked like he was going to fall off. He had hold of the horn on the saddle and the reins. His mule wasn't as big as mine, and Gabe was big. His shoulders were broad. He looked like a scared giant sitting on that mule. I got to laughing and almost fell off my mule.

Gabe frowned at me and shook his head. We made our way down into the canyon. I looked around so I would recognize my surroundings and was amazed by the beauty. The different colors of the canyon kept me enthralled. It seemed like everywhere I looked, it was different. I thought this would be a nice place to visit with Gilly.

We had been riding for about three hours. My ass hurt like hell, and I wanted a giant hamburger and Pepsi. I looked behind me at Gabe and thought he was sleeping. What if he fell over the edge of the canyon? I stopped my mule. "Gabe." He jumped and almost fell off. "Stay awake." He nodded.

And we kept going. I was ready to fall off the mule when we reached the bottom. I climbed off, and my legs buckled. I heard Gabe laugh and watched him get off his mule. His legs buckled. Both of us sat there for a few minutes then we got up. Believe me. It was hard pulling ourselves up. Damn hard. I could barely walk. We both knew what we had to do. We had to work the stiffness out of our legs.

"We'll be back. We have to run for a few miles."

"Watch for snakes."

We ran for an hour and then watched the Colorado river go by. I stripped out of my clothes and jumped in. Gabe did the same thing. The water was like ice. I barely kept from shouting, it was so cold. I saw the man when I was getting out of the water. He had a grin on his face looking at us. Gabe and I climbed out and got dressed. He watched us the entire time.

"Who you two be?"

"Who you be?" I asked in return.

"My name is Coyote. I live down here at the bottom of the canyon. Are you the men that will stop the killing and the thievery of my family's artifacts?"

"Yes, I hope we can stop it. I thought only Indians lived down here?"

"Nope, I was raised by the Dakota people. I have never lived anywhere else. Now they have people coming here to murder other White people. I think it's a White man doing it."

"Why do you think that?"

"Because the White man is obsessed with our artifacts. We don't like them coming here and destroying our land with garbage. The stories passed down from generation to generation are not pretty. The federal government does nothing to clean up after them. The people who live here clean up everything."

"Do you think the Indians are killing and stealing, trying to scare people?"

"No, we know it's not them. These artifacts belong to the nations here. There are eleven nations from the Grand

Canyon. It's the White man who is doing this. We have tried catching them, but another man was murdered. I hope that you find whoever is doing this. We have put others to guard the artifacts."

"We'll see you around Coyote, be careful walking around here alone."

"I will be. I don't want to startle you, but you almost stepped on that rattler by your foot."

I jumped backward, tripped over a boulder, and landed on my butt. The snake was almost in my lap when Gabe kicked it, and it flew into the air far away from me. "Thanks, that was scary." My heart was beating so fast that I took a moment before I stood up.

24

GILLY

I met Hannah at the shop at six a.m. She was excited to become the manager of the coffee shop. Mace was not happy. He thought Hannah should stay home with the girls. But since they were living with his mom, Debra, Hannah didn't have to worry about them. Debra and Mace wanted the girls close to them.

Hannah had money from her house that burned down in Montana but she said she needed to get away from Mace for a while each day. She said Mace oozes sex off his body, and he decided they would be friends, not lovers. Mace got Hannah's horses over here, and she is boarding them out on a ranch here. Hannah is a cowgirl.

"Why don't you make him jealous? How long have you been here?"

"Seven months. I've tried everything to get his juices flowing. One morning, I answered the door in my panties and tank top, hoping to make him take me in his arms and throw me on the bed. It was Ryker and Mace. Mace growled, and I giggled."

I couldn't hold it in. I laughed. "What did he say?"

"He asked if I planned to stand there naked all day for Ryker to ogle me. Ryker burst into laughter, and I giggled as I ran to my room. Who could I use to make Mace jealous?"

"Are you kidding me? Open your eyes. There are so many handsome men around. All you have to do is ask them. They would love holding you in their arms. How about Blade? You have to admit he is hotter than an inferno."

"I don't know. Blade is kind of scary. He looks so dangerous when he turns that smile on you."

"Only if he is angry with you."

"I went to a club one night with Darcy, and he was there. This man wouldn't leave us alone. We were getting ready to leave when the man blocked our way. Blade was there so fast he looked at us and smiled that smile. Then he turned, and the next thing I knew, the guy was knocked out on the floor. Blade told us goodnight, and we left."

"Okay. How about Jackson? He is perfect. He's playful and handsome, plus he would love doing this. I'll talk to him."

"Are you sure? What if it backfires?"

"It won't. We both know Mace doesn't know what the hell to do. You told me what happened at the Marriott when he got you out of prison. He must be afraid to love again. He was destroyed for years, and you brought him out of that. He has strong feelings for you. You'll see."

"I want someone who loves me as much as he loves someone who isn't here. I don't want him if Mace can't love me that much. Knowing his mind was on her, I would always be sad, knowing he felt guilty for being with me."

"I understand completely. You deserve the best kind of love."

"I'm glad we became friends. Lucy wants me to go to school and be a nurse."

"What do you want to do?"

"I've been looking into it. I haven't decided yet. When you have three little girls, it's hard to leave them. I love them so much. I had no one. My family was killed in an accident, and I was left alone. Then I met Mace, and God gave me my beautiful girls."

I turned my head and saw Mace standing there.

"God gave both of us beautiful girls. I want them to see you when they wake up in the mornings. I don't want you to work."

"I know you don't. I'm only working until noon, and then I'll go home to our girls."

I could see the fight within Mace's eyes, it looked like he wanted to say more, but something or someone was holding him back. Maybe he would figure it out on his own sooner or later. But Hannah needs him to be now.

"Here you go," I said, handing him a cup of coffee. He took it and left. "I'll be there when the girls wake up. I know you have a life beyond the girls. You need to get out sometimes and do whatever you want to do. You have that right. I'm sorry I'm being selfish."

"No, you are not. You're a good father who is concerned about his girls. That reminds me, I have a date on Saturday. Can the girls sleep at your house that night?"

"What do you mean you have a date? Who do you have a date with? Never mind, you don't have to tell me."

"I don't mind. I have a date with Blade."

"Blade. Are you telling me Blade fucking asked you out on a date?"

"Umm, yeah."

Mace turned and stormed out of the coffee shop. Jackson stood there watching him.

"You do know he's going straight to Blade's house."

"What am I going to do?" Hannah cried. "He was so angry."

"He was jealous," Jackson said.

"I have to call Blade. Do you have his phone number?"

"Yes…" Hannah got the phone number and hit the buttons. "I don't even know him. What do I say?"

"Just tell me what you want to."

"I put him on speaker," Hannah said.

"Is this some kind of kinky sex thing?" Blade asked over the speaker.

"No!"

Hannah handed me the phone. I started talking in a hurry telling him before Mace got there. "Blade, Hannah tried to make Mace jealous. And he might be on his way to see you. He was angrier than we thought he would be."

"What do I have to do with Mace and Hannah besides him sending me to keep an eye on her when she goes out with Darcy."

"She told him she had a date with you on Saturday night to make him jealous so he would make a move. Hell, she's been here for seven months. I'm afraid it was my idea. Mace is angry."

"I'm not home now, but I'll see Hannah on Saturday at seven." Then he hung up.

25

MACE

I decided not to say anything to Blade. Damn him. I couldn't believe he was taking Hannah out on a date. Damn him. I should bust his head open for doing this. I walked over to Mom's, and Hannah and the girls were in the bedroom. Hannah was putting lip gloss on or some kind of lip stuff.

"You look beautiful as always. Where are you going?"

"We're going to dinner."

"Who wants to stay at Daddy's tonight?"

All three of the girls yelled, "I do," as I knew they would. Hannah stood up and picked up her jacket.

"Here, I'll put it on for you." I could feel her shaking. She wanted me as much as I wanted her. Now, what was she going to do? Have that damn smooth-talking Blade making love to her?

I stepped back and away from her. "Come along girls. We need to start dinner. We'll have grandma come to dinner with us. Who wants spaghetti?"

"I do."

"Me too."

"I do."

"I'll take some of that spaghetti," my mom said, walking down the hall. She looked into the bedroom, "Wow, someone is going to have a good time tonight. I've known Blade a long time, and the Blade I know will try to make a move on the first date. So you be on the lookout for those hands of his."

Hannah giggled and stood up as the doorbell rang. "He's early," Hannah said, smiling as she stood up.

I walked behind her as she opened the door. I wanted Blade to know he was messing with the wrong man's property. Why the hell would I think that? *Hannah is no one's property. She belongs to only herself. And she was smiling at Blade. I wanted her to smile at me the way she was smiling at him.*

"You look beautiful," Blade said, kissing her lips lightly.

"Thank you. You look pretty beautiful yourself." He chuckled as he slipped his arm around her.

"Goodbye, girls. I will see you in the morning."

"How will you see them in the morning if you are at work?"

"I don't work weekends."

"Why does that man have his arm around Mommy?" Annie asked the room.

I watched as Blade guided her to his vehicle. His hand was down low on her back. I wanted to break those fingers. I'm sure I would have a fight on my hands, trying to break his fingers. They didn't call Blade Lethal Blade for no reason.

"Why is Mommy getting in that man's car?" Annie continued asking questions as we walked to my house. "Did that man just now kiss Mommy again?" I heard my mom chuckle. I didn't see anything funny about the situation.

"Your mommy is going on a date with Blade. They are going to dinner. I'm sure the kiss didn't mean anything," my mom tried explaining. Annie was still not pleased with her mommy going on a date.

"But we have our Daddy. Mommy should go to dinner with Daddy?"

"Your Daddy hasn't asked her to go to dinner."

"Why?"

"Annie, enough with the questions." I knew the moment I spoke, it was too rough. But damn it, I was angry.

"Sorry," she said. Her head was bent, and her lip trembled.

I picked her up and kissed her. "I'm sorry for being mean. Do you forgive me?"

"Yes, Daddy. I wouldn't ever go out to dinner with a man. Only my Daddy. I love you, Daddy."

"I love you, sweetie."

"I love you too, Daddy."

"I love you too, Daddy."

"I love all three of you more than anything in the world." Having triplets, I've learned to wait until all of them have finished talking, or I would be answering their questions all night.

I was awake at twelve when Blade brought Hannah home. I saw her hesitate as to where she wanted to sleep. I knew she wanted to be with the girls but didn't know what to do. I opened the back door, so she would see me. She didn't hesitate. She ran over and walked inside.

"Can I sleep in one of your tee shirts, please?"

"I walked into my room and grabbed her something. I handed her the shirt and watched as she turned her back, slipped out of her dress, and then her bra. She pulled the shirt over her head. My cock was rock hard. I wanted her under me naked, but I would never hurt her because I would never get married again. I loved Monica, and I loved my boys, Mason and Anthony. I could never go through that pain again. I contemplated suicide so many times during those years. I don't know what would have happened if Mom hadn't had that heart attack and needed me.

"Goodnight."

"Goodnight." I watched her walk into the bedroom where the girls slept. I had put four twin beds in there. I had wanted them to always stay at my house because it was now their home. I had two extra bedrooms added onto the house. But the girls wanted to sleep in the same room with each other. So I put four beds in there.

I have remodeled it since the girls and Hannah walked into my life. I bought the vacant property next door and was building a barn and corrals for Hannah's horses. It was to be a surprise, but Annie told her about it.

26

GILLY

Gray sent me some more beautiful photos of the Canyon, with the sun coming up. I texted him, 'This is beautiful. Thank you for sharing all these photos and videos. When are you coming home?'

'I don't know yet. As soon as we catch the killer and thief. I can't wait to see you. I love you.'

'I love you too. I miss you,' I texted as I walked into the coffee shop.

"Why are you awake this early?" Hannah asked, as I walked to the counter.

"I'm an early bird."

"Yes, but you have been working so hard at the boatyard. That place is looking good."

"Thank you. I want to get it cleaned up before I check to see how salvageable those boats are. The man whose family owned it for over a hundred years has been coming every morning. I'm going to bring him coffee and donuts. How's it going making Mace jealous?"

"I've been on two dates. The next time, I will tell Blade to keep me out later. Or maybe an all-nighter. Mace was awake both times, waiting for me. He would open the back door for me to come inside and sleep with the girls. He doesn't seem to be jealous. The first night I stepped out of my dress, my back was turned I put his tee shirt on to sleep in. He did nothing."

"It's only two dates. What does Blade say about all of this?"

"He's getting into making Mace jealous too. He kisses me when he picks me up, so Mace can see what he's missing. That's what he told me when I asked about him kissing me."

I chuckled. "Blade likes kissing you for more reasons than making Mace jealous. I hope he's not becoming attached to you."

"He would never become attached to me or any woman. He has more girlfriends than anyone I know. I think something happened when he was younger. I asked him, and he looked at me like I was crazy. I'll do this for a little bit longer. If Mace isn't jealous, I'll have to think of something else."

"Good, then I'm off."

"I'll see you around."

I made my way down to the waterfront, the sun was coming up, and I sat the coffee and donuts down and took a video. I sent it to Gray with a text, 'We will see this every morning when you get home.'

'What if we don't want to get out of bed? I can think of many reasons to stay in bed with you.'

'Well, there is that. Maybe not every morning.' I sighed, thinking about what we could do to stay in bed. 'Come home soon. I love you.'

'I love you too, sweetheart.'

I walked into the office at the boatyard and handed Joe his coffee and donut. I would be getting fat if I kept this up.

"Look, I thought there was something I wanted to tell you. See these papers here?"

"Yes."

"They are a deed to that property next door. They go with the deal we made. I thought there was something else. But I couldn't remember."

"Let's go look at it." We walked outside, and I looked at the vacant lot. That lot is also yours. But I was talking about that lot, he said, pointing at the Victorian house sitting on the lot where the flowers grew wild and rose bushes sprang up everywhere.

I went to grab hold of something before I fell. There was nothing to hold, so my butt hit the ground.

"Are you okay?"

"Yes."

Joe looked down at me. "Do you want to take a look at it?"

"Yes."

I got up, and we walked up to the front porch. "Be careful. This old thing looks like it's going to fall apart."

"It's beautiful. How come you don't live here?"

"My wife never liked anything to do with the boatyard. I hate to admit this out loud for the first time. My wife loved my brother. They were going to be married. I've always loved her. My brother died at sea. She almost committed suicide, and that's when she found out she was going to have a child.

"The baby she was carrying brought her back to life. I asked her to marry me. She said yes, because of the baby. We were married and lived in this house until Mary fell down these stairs and lost the baby. We moved out, and no one has lived here since. I would come and stay a few days just to get drunk.

"My life was working at the boatyard, and now it will all be back to its glorious self. My life was miserable because my wife wouldn't even talk to me. You are the only one I've ever told that story to. The house can be a happy place again, with you, Grayson, and your children. You and Grayson should get started on that family to fill up all these rooms."

We walked inside the house, and I could only stare; my mouth hung open. The place looked like I had gone back in time. Everything must have been like it was that day so many years ago. Joe sat at the dining room table, drinking his coffee and eating his donut as I walked into every room of this beautiful home—some of the wood needed to be replaced in the flooring. I could do that on my own. A window upstairs was broken, but the frame was still in perfect shape. I would replace all the windows with storm windows but keep them in the same frames. Wow, I couldn't wait for Gray to get home.

I decided right then to move into this house. I ran downstairs, where Joe sat eating his donut. "Take us to the lawyers. I want to ensure everything is in your and Gray's name."

"Who is the lawyer?"

"I use Mace when I can track him down. Now that he has those little girls, he'll stay put."

We drove to Mace's home, where he was outside, building the barn with other men. I knew right then he had bought that property and planned on surprising Hannah. Joe hurried to where he was and talked for a few minutes, and then Mace walked over to me. He was shirtless, and I saw the tattoo down his back. It said the only loves of my life are Monica, Mason, and Anthony.

"Shouldn't you add Annie, Abby, and Ellie?"

"What?"

"On your back. It says the only loves of my life are Monica, Mason, and Anthony. Are you concerned that the girls will be hurt because their names aren't on your back? What if you fall in love again, and your new lady sees your back? When did you put that tattoo on your body?" I knew I was becoming angry for my friend and the girls. We were here for something else. I should just shut up.

"Why is it any of your business?"

"Because Hannah and the girls are close to me. I don't want to see them hurt."

"The girls are too young to understand what the meaning is. Don't worry about my family."

"Your family. Wouldn't you have their names tattooed onto your body if you thought of them as your family? You deliberately had that tattoo put on your back for Hannah to see. You thought she would fall in love with you and wanted to ensure that never happened."

"You don't know what you are talking about."

"Don't I? Then let the girls see it and see if Annie doesn't ask you why their names are not tattooed on you?" I looked at Joe, "I can't be in the same space as Mace right now. You two do this, and he can bring you back to the boatyard."

"I don't know why you are getting so damn angry over this," Mace said, standing in my path.

"I'll tell you why I'm angry. Hannah is sweet and honest and would never hurt a living soul. But you did this to hurt her."

"I did this to remind myself never to let myself fall in love again. I never want to go through that again."

"I'm sure you won't ever have to worry about it with that tattoo on you. Now, get out of my fucking way."

"Daddy," Annie called out as the three girls approached

us. Then I saw his mom walking to us. I knew Mace wanted to wear his shirt, but it was at the barn.

"Hannah, Joe, you must come over for coffee."

"I've already had my coffee, thank you. Next time for sure," I said as I turned to leave. "I'll see you around," I said, walking away.

"I'll go with you," Joe said.

Joe looked at me when we got in the car. "That will take some explaining. Now that little girl can stop going out with Blade to make Mace jealous."

"I swear I'm so angry with Mace. How could he do something like that?"

"You would have to have known Mace in his first life. His family was his life. He and those boys did everything together. They would go fishing all the time. He loved them so much. I look at Mace as his first life and his second life. Plus, the in-between life. That man was a stranger to all who knew him."

"When his boys died, he died. The entire town mourned the death of them boys. His wife, I believe she had problems with depression. This angry person who hated everything was in Mace's place. He didn't like the sun coming up or the sun going down. He used women, but they loved being used by him. Every once in a while, I would see the real Mace, so I was hopeful that one day he would return.

"It went on for years. He would just disappear. Once, he was gone for an entire year. I think that must have been when he met Hannah and the babies were created. I like to think of them as something God gave to both of them. He wanted Hannah to have someone to love and who loved her back, and he wanted Mace to have someone to save him."

"I think you are right. So what is Mace going to do about that damn tattoo?"

"He will have to admit he made a horrible mistake and put every one of their names on his body. If I were him, I would have their name over my heart. What do you think?"

"I think I could listen to you talking all day long. I'm glad we are friends. I couldn't do the boatyard without you helping me. Plus, you can tell a story and make me feel as if I was right there with them. And damn, I'm going to cry," I said, wiping my eyes. "Mace has been hit from everywhere. I'm glad I didn't know mister in-between."

"Everyone who knew him tried fixing him one way or another. I believe he has gotten into a fight with every one of his Seal buddies. When his mama had her heart attack, it took a while for his friends to find him. He came home but still hung out with some nasty characters—motorcycle gangs.

"He finally saw what it was doing to Debra and straightened up. He sold his and Monica's home and bought the one he's at now. I'm only telling you this, so you will understand what he went through. He and Monica were childhood sweethearts. But just between us, I always thought he loved Monica because that's how he always felt about her.

"He has always loved her. But what he feels for Hannah is powerful. He feels guilty because he loves her more and in a different way than he loved Monica. With Hannah, his body and his mind betray him because he can't control his feelings."

"I hope he manages to sort everything out before he runs Hannah off. I know she wouldn't go far, maybe a town over from here, just so she's not in the same yard as him."

"I hope so too. So what do we want to tackle first?"

"Let's tackle the house. I know you want to get moved into it. I had the utilities turned on, and while you choose a room you want to start on, I will make sure the fireplaces are cleaned out."

"Why don't you choose a room, and you can move in here with Gray and me. It'll be like a bed and breakfast. I'm a pretty good cook. But I think Gray is a much better cook than me. Did he ever tell you the story of how we met?"

"Yes, you were his wrong date. He told me about the woman who was obsessed with vinegar. We laughed for hours over that woman's cooking. Maybe I will stay with you. I'll take the bedroom behind the kitchen. It's the one I used to take when I would stay away from my wife for a few days."

Two days later, we were all moved into the rooms we chose. I picked the main bedroom even though the plumbing wasn't that great. It would do for now. Later down the road, we could upgrade it. I wanted to surprise Gray, so I didn't mention it in our text back and forth with each other in the early mornings while the sun was rising. I missed my man, and that is what he is. He's mine, and I love him so much.

27

GRAY

I could have sworn I heard something. I stepped to the side, and a damn arrow flew past my head. "Gabe, watch out! Someone is shooting arrows at us." They knew we were getting close to discovering who the killer and the thief were. All four of us got behind a boulder.

"So I take it this means it's an Indian," one of the guides said.

"No, someone could be trying to make us believe it's an Indian." There that noise was again. We all looked at each other and knew it was a rattlesnake. This was like the tenth rattler I'd seen. Only I didn't see this one. I heard it. I looked around. Then one of the guides pointed down, and I almost fainted. It was a bed of rattlers curled up at the bottom of the rock. I would rather be hit with an arrow than be bitten by a bunch of snakes.

Let me tell you how I became scared of snakes. When I was eleven, I went camping with Gabe's family. There are four boys in Gabe's family, and I must admit the two older ones always tried to make our lives miserable. They've played tricks on us since I was around four. This time, it backfired on them. Jack had found a snake, and they decided to see if they could catch it and throw it on Gabe and me. We were way up in the mountains. We had hiked two miles up from where we had left the car.

I was sitting around the fire when they threw this snake at me. I jumped up and screamed, and the snake landed in their dad's lap. I watched as the rattlesnake went to bite their dad. He grabbed it and threw it into the fire.

When it landed in the fire, it somehow made its way out while it was on fire. It started chasing Jack and Jake, the pranksters. They were running in a circle screaming when Gabe smashed its head with his boot. He picked it up by the tail and threw it back into the fire. That night and many more after that, I would have these nightmares about rattlesnakes. I've been scared of them ever since. And now here I am with a bed of the damn things ready to strike.

I grabbed my gun, jumped out behind the rock, and fired my weapon. I heard someone cry out, and then I heard someone running. I took off after them. The guy I hit lay on the ground crying. I jumped over him and ran. I knew I would catch this guy. I run every morning ten miles a day.

I knew Gabe would get the other guy. And now all I had to do was catch this guy, and I could go home to Gilly. The thing with me and running was that I planned everything in my head while running.

I knew the guy was getting tired. He was slowing down. He wouldn't go much further. At the same time, I was in my head planning. He threw something. I knew what it was the moment I saw it. I jumped to the side, but it still got me. I was pissed. I aimed my gun and shot the bastard as he checked to see if I was dead.

I was taking deep breaths trying to stay awake. I didn't want to pass out; I needed to tell Gabe something. FUCK!

Why did this happen? I didn't want to die. But I knew if I didn't get to the hospital fast, I would.

Gilly, I love you. I will always love you here on earth or in heaven. You will always be with me.

"Fuck, I thought that was a grenade."

"Gabe, I need you to tell Gilly I'm sorry this happened. Tell her how much I love her."

"You tell her when she visits you in the hospital. You're not going to die; I won't let you. Do you hear me? Fuck, did he just die?"

∽

Gabe

"Get back so I can take care of him." The guide didn't waste time talking. He cut Gray out his clothes while the other handed him things from his black bag.

"Are you guys doctors?"

"Surgeons. But we are also guides. It frees my mind if I get out of the hospital."

"Yeah, mine too," the other guide said.

I went and checked on the man that Gray shot. He was dead. I kicked him to make sure. He looked familiar. I remembered seeing him at the hotel. I think he worked on the city council. So they hired us, but they planned on killing us. That didn't make sense. I'd figure it out later. We had to save Gray now. I heard the copter and turned. He was landing. Why the hell didn't we have a helicopter in the first place?

I returned to where they were patching Gray for the hospital ride. Is that a damn snake bite? I said, looking closely at his back. The doctor, who was a guide, looked at it, grabbed something out of his bag, and gave Gray a shot.

"What's that?"

"Snake venom. He might have landed close to a rattlesnake or on one."

The hand grenade tore his back up. The surgeon was pulling pieces of his clothing from the wound on his back. I saw him give Gray another shot. "What's that for?" I asked.

"To keep him sleeping. We have to get him to the hospital quick."

Three hours later, I was sitting in the waiting room when a white face Gilly hurried into the room, followed by Ryker and Lincoln.

"What happened to him?" Gilly demanded.

I am a straight talker. I told her what I knew. "This guy threw a grenade at him. He jumped out of its main path, but it got him. Then while he was on the ground, before we got there, a rattlesnake bit him. Our guides down into the canyon happened to be surgeons. I don't know anything else." I turned and looked at Gilly, "Gilly, Gray wanted me to tell you he's sorry about this happening and that he loves you more than anything."

"So where is most of the damage on his body? Maybe it stayed away from his main arteries, lungs, and other organs."

"It mostly got the backside of him. I know he lost a lot of blood; hopefully, that wasn't coming from any arteries. We have to wait and see what happens. I know he will fight like hell to live. He loves you too much to die."

Ryker hugged her, and then he looked at me, "Fill me in on what the hell happened?"

"The guy who threw the grenade worked on the city council. His buddy confessed everything. He said he was hired to steal the artifacts and kill those people. A couple of other council members were in on it as well. They didn't think it was right for the artifacts to be down in the canyon, wasting away. He thought he could sell them."

"Bastards, if Gray dies, I'll hang all of them by their balls and let the Indians take care of them. So they picked a few tourists who they decided they could kill."

"That's about it."

28

GILLY

I paced the hallway waiting for the surgeon to tell us about Gray. We've been here for two hours already. Gray was in surgery for three hours before we got here. What the hell was taking them so long?

I walked back to the waiting room, and the surgeon was already there. I stepped inside.

"The doctor just arrived, Gilly."

"So, you're Gilly. Gray told me all about you when we were in the canyon. You take beautiful photos. I was a little jealous of how much you two loved each other. It must be a peaceful feeling knowing someone loves you as much as you love them."

"Yes, it is. How is Gray?"

"He'll have scars and be grumpy for a couple of months because he'll have to sleep on his stomach. We were able to give him the snake venom in time. He might have bite marks on his side for a while but will live a long, happy life. He'll have to take time off his job for a while. Some of those wounds go deep, and we don't want anything interfering with his recovery."

I started crying. I held my hands over my face and couldn't stop crying. I was a mess. I talked while my hands were still over my face. "When can I see Gray?"

"He'll be taken to ICU. Give it thirty minutes."

I threw my arms around the doctor, blubbering like an idiot to him. "Thank you for being their guide while they were in the canyon. Gabe told us if you weren't there, Gray would have died."

"Yeah, what is strange is that it wasn't our turn to guide. Jeff called and said he needed a break. He was going to see if we could switch with someone. The guides which usually went both had called in with the flu."

"God put you there to take care of Gray. Thank you."

"You're welcome. Give the staff thirty minutes."

I nodded and looked at the guys. They all had grins on their faces. "What do I look like, a raccoon with makeup running down my face?"

"Yes, you do," Gabe said, smiling.

I gave them twenty-seven minutes before I went in to see Gray. He lay on his stomach, his back uncovered so they could keep an eye on it. His side and shoulder were also injured. I looked over his body. I kissed every wound. I heard a chuckle.

"That better be my lady kissing me, or you'll have to answer to Gilly."

"Grayson Campbell. It's a good thing you are going to live. I would have died right along with you. I love you so much," I told him, then I started crying.

"You'll have to leave. You're upsetting the other patients."

"If she leaves, I leave; put me in a private room."

"I'll talk to your doctor."

"Gilly, sweetheart. I'm going to be okay. I don't want you to worry."

"I know. I'm so emotional lately. I'm sorry for crying. I was so scared. Remember I told you I have a surprise?"

"Yes."

"You know that Victorian house on the waterfront?"

"Yes."

"It's ours."

"What do you mean?"

"Joe said it goes with the deal we made. No one has lived in it for a long time. But I've been cleaning our room. I let Joe move into a room also."

"What about my modern home? Don't you like it?"

"Of course, I do. I'm sorry, I should have said I moved into the old house. You, of course, can stay in your home. There I go again, jumping to conclusions." He opened his eyes and smiled.

"I love you, Gillian Marshall. When are we going to get married?"

"Oh, no, I'm going to cry again. We will get married soon." He closed his eyes and went to sleep. I wiped my eyes and walked into the waiting room, "Gray is going to be okay. We are getting married soon. Wow, I'm turning into a crybaby."

"Thank God he's going to be okay," Gabe said. "How does he look?"

"He looks wonderful. His back, side, and shoulder are pretty bad, but what is important is that he will live and be a healthy man after he recovers from his injuries. They'll be putting him into his own room soon."

"We are going to be heading back to Oregon. Are you staying here?"

"Yes, I'm not going home without Gray. I'll wait here if anyone wants to see him before you leave." They all decided to visit him before they left. Then I went and sat next to him.

I carried my travel bag and Gray's bag with me. I was sleeping in the chair when my eyes opened, and Gray stared at me.

"Sweetheart, come and lay beside me."

"No, I don't want to hurt you."

"You aren't going to hurt me."

I walked over to where he was and climbed in beside him. I kissed his lips, and all sorts of noises went off. The nurse came running into our cubicle.

"I'm sorry, but you will have to move from the bed. You're messing the monitors up."

I smiled at Gray. "We got caught with our hand in the cookie jar." I kissed him and moved.

"We are just waiting for an orderly to move him to a private room. They are putting another bed in there for you. We know you live in Oregon. Besides, I think if you lived down the street, you would still stay here."

"You're right. I would. Thank you for understanding."

"I was young once upon a time."

I looked at Gray, and he was sleeping. The more he slept, the faster he would get better. I sat back down in the chair. I checked my email and did other mundane things until the orderly showed up to move him.

I followed with our bags. The room was big, and when I opened the curtains, the desert was the view. It was nice for a hospital room. I saw the bed they gave me and put our bags on it. "I have never lived with a man before. The only man I have ever loved will be the first and last man I ever live with."

"That's good to know, sweetheart."

"I'm sorry, I didn't realize I was talking out loud."

"Lay down next to me. Did you pick a day?"

"Not yet. I've only had a couple of hours to think about

it. I say the sooner, the better. I don't have to have a fancy wedding—just our friends and family."

"That sounds perfect. How about a month from now?"

"If you are ready by then, I love that day..." I must have fallen asleep because Gray's family was there when I woke up.

"Hello, Gilly. Did we wake you?"

"No, I'm sorry; I fell asleep." I got up and ran my fingers through my tangles.

Hutch smiled. "You don't have anything to be sorry for. I hear there is going to be a wedding."

"Yes, I'm so excited. I smiled at Gray's mom. You probably are constantly on edge with these two boys."

"Yes, I am. I bet your mom was the same with you, always out on those rigs trying to fix them."

"Well, I never told my mom how dangerous my job was. She mostly just knew I was out at sea a lot."

"Gray tells us you want a small wedding with family and friends. I've always thought those are the best weddings. I saw the work you've done at the boatyard. It's really coming along. I talked to Joe. He seems happier than he's ever been. He's a good man who got stuck in a marriage from hell."

"I always wondered about his marriage. So I guess it was just as my mother said. He married the wrong woman."

"Who never spoke a word to him their entire marriage..." I looked at Gray, and he smiled at me. "I want you to know I love Gray more than anything in this world, and I will always talk to him."

Gray and Hutch started laughing. "Even when he doesn't want you to," Hutch said.

"Yes, even then."

29

GRAY

My back was almost completely healed. I was ready to marry the woman of my dreams, and she was working her butt off at the boatyard. I tried slowing her down, but she wanted our wedding to be held here. I watched her walking. Her limp was completely gone, stretching her muscles did the job.

I saw her sister and her girls here almost every day. Gilly filled me in on what was happening with Adam's father. Apparently, all this time, it was that photo that Lucy had taken that they needed to arrest the man, and then Adam went through all his papers and found the proof they needed.

Adam was still trying to find proof that he had killed his mother. That was something Adam couldn't get out of his system. Then while in court, his father confronted him.

"You have always had it in for me. But I never thought my son would work with the feds to put me away for life."

"And I would never have thought my father would do the things you've done. You killed my mother, you bastard."

"You were better off without her. All she did was nag."

"You bastard," Adam charged the guy, and a woman with him at the courthouse shot and killed his father. Her name was Dakota Suneagle. She was once one of those trafficked women.

I was glad Adam was free of that man. I watched as Adam carried the youngest child, she wasn't Adam's daughter, but to Adam, these girls were his. Lucy's baby would be here in a couple of months, and she and Adam were getting married again. They both got their second chance.

I saw Mace walking toward me, and he wasn't smiling. "What?"

"Tell Gilly not to be setting my wife... I mean, the girls' mother up on dates with Blade."

"Gilly didn't set her up with him. Blade has a thing for Hannah."

"What do you mean a thing?"

"You should have claimed pretty Hannah the day you rescued her. The guys thought she was your woman until they saw you out with Sharon. So it would be best if you talked to Blade, not me. I want you, the girls, and your mom here for my wedding."

"We'll be here."

"Day after tomorrow at noon."

"I know."

Mace walked off, and I walked to where my beautiful bride-to-be was. "You look gorgeous out here with sweat glistening on your body. I'm hotter than hell. Is there any way we can ditch these people and play in the shower?"

Gilly laughed, "Why yes, I believe there is a way." She turned to her sister, "Gray and I are going to go play in the shower. You all can go home and play in your own shower."

I saw Lucy take Adam's hand, and they walked to their

vehicle and left. "Follow me, husband-to-be. We are going to make a mess of the bathroom floor."

"Which bathroom are we going to?"

"The modern one. It has more hot water."

"And water pressure. I'll talk to a plumber. If we live at the Victorian, the plumbing must be updated. I must tell you, sweetheart. I like all the modern devices we have in this age. I'm sure I'll be fine once we get the plumbing fixed. Are we changing the color of the house?"

"No way! I am keeping that beautiful pink color." We went back and forth the way we always did about the old house. I loved that home I always had growing up. I always wanted to see inside of it. Now we own it. Or we will once we get it paid off. Joe lived with us. I was happy he did because he was tired and wanted to sleep most of the time. Gilly always made sure he ate good meals.

When we made it to the bathroom, we were already naked. Gilly kissed all my wounds like she always did when I was naked. The snake bite marks were still visible. I followed her into the shower and picked up the soap. I started lathering her, and then she lathered me. We were both getting hotter than hell. I pushed my two fingers in between her hot folds.

Gilly was riding my hand as I gave her what she wanted. She orgasmed, and I lifted her and let her body slide down until I slid inside her.

We were wild, like every time we made love. I knew it would always be like this with Gilly

"Let's take a nap, sweetheart."

"What kind of nap?"

"You know what kind? The I'll be tasting you all over kind," I said, carrying her to the bed. We made hot, sweaty, sticky love for an hour, then we fell asleep.

THE WEATHER WAS beautiful on our wedding day, and birds were singing. Hutch was my best man, and Lucy was Gilly's maid of honor. Gilly cried the entire time. She said she was so happy, she had to cry. Her sister cried, her mother cried, and even Hannah cried. I looked at my mom and sister, and they were also crying. So, I guess when they say everyone cries at weddings, it is because they are so happy. That is why I cried at my wedding.

The food was delicious, and I almost started crying again when Hutch toasted us. He shared his memory of the day I met Gilly and how often he and our buddies had to listen to the story of my wrong date.

When Lucy toasted, she told the story of when Gilly met her wrong date and everything she had said about me being her soul mate, and she knew we would find each other again. Because soul mates fall in love only once, and that is with their soul mate. I was almost crying again, listening to how Gilly thought of us. We both knew we belonged together and would spend the rest of our lives together.

"So I toast my sister and my new brother who has found true love. Sometimes you think you love someone, and you do love them, but they are not your true love. Your true love makes your heart hurt when you think of them. They make you want to cry thinking of them. I'm so happy that Gray and Gilly will be crying together for the rest of their lives."

Everyone laughed, and then the guys toasted us, saying how tired they were of hearing about my wrong date. I looked at Gilly. She was watching me.

I toasted my bride, "To the woman I love and wasn't afraid to tell the world how I felt, even if they were tired of hearing me say it. My father knew about Gilly before he died. He told me, 'Go find your Gilly and let the world know you love her.'" I leaned over to Gilly, "This is the best day of my life. Thank you for marrying me, sweetheart," I whispered in her ear.

I love you." She kissed me on my neck, where I knew there was a scar.

30

MACE

This tattoo I had reminded me not to tell Hannah how I felt about her. I had one wife, and I didn't need another one. I couldn't go through what I went through. This time, I knew it would kill me.

A week had passed since the wedding. I was helping in the barn, shirtless, and forgot about the damn tattoo. The kids ran over to me, and my mom and Hannah followed them. "Daddy painted his back again." That's when I remembered the tattoo.

"Did you get a new tattoo?" Mom asked. I walked to where my shirt was, but she was already reading it. "The only woman I will ever love is Monica Cohen, the mother of my beautiful sons Mason and Anthony." My mom was shaking her head.

I looked at Hannah. I couldn't tell what she thought or felt. Her face was expressionless.

"Who is that?" Annie asked. They waited for me to explain since I was the one to let the world know about them with this tattoo.

"I used to have two little boys. They were killed in an accident."

"Were they with their mommy?"

"Yes."

"Are you going to put our names on you too?"

"Do you want me to?"

"Yes, I want you to put it right here," she said, putting her hand over my heart.

"Then that's what I will do."

"We came to tell you we are back from shopping," Mom said. She looked like she might cry.

"Come along, girls. We need to get dinner started," Hannah said, taking Abby's hand.

I watched as they walked away. I knew what my mom was going to say before she said it.

"Once you put a tattoo on you, it will forever be there. Why did you have that tattoo put on? What about Hannah? I know you love her. You should open your eyes before it's too late if it's not already," and then she turned to walk away.

"I'm scared, Mom. I don't know what to do. I love Hannah, damn it. I don't want to feel these feelings again. This time, it's more powerful than it's ever been. I did love Monica. I've always loved her since we were children, you know that. I loved her with my whole heart. But what I feel for Hannah, I know I would never get over it. I can't take that chance that something will happen to her."

"Then you can say goodbye to Hannah because she won't stay here after this. She is a proud woman. Too proud, maybe. She won't wait for you to do something, and she won't make the first move. When you put that tattoo on your body, to her, you made your decision. She's been here almost a year, and you haven't let her know how you feel about her one way or another. If you don't fix this, it'll be too late."

Two days later, I still didn't know what to do. I walked into my mom's, and it was so quiet. "Where is everyone?"

"Hannah was meeting a contractor back home. She said she's going to get started building before winter gets here."

"What? She took my girls away. How could she do that? When did they leave?"

"They went out to dinner with Blade. See how it would be without Hannah and the girls?"

"I can't believe they all went to dinner with Blade."

"They went to the rodeo. He knows how much Hannah loves her horses."

"You think I don't know? I'm building her a frigging barn. I don't like her taking the girls around him."

"They will be okay with Blade. You don't have to worry about them getting hurt around him. He'll keep a close eye on those girls, all four of them."

I didn't know if mom was putting digs in on purpose or if she just didn't understand how much it bothered me. I showered and then made my way out to my truck. Those are my girls. If someone were taking them to the rodeo, it should be me.

I drove over to the next town to the rodeo. I was walking around and spotted Blade right away. He stood over most of the people there. I made my way to them and saw people looking into the arena. I heard Annie shouting for her mommy. The girls' faces looked like they didn't know what would happen. I turned my head and saw Hannah going as fast as she could on a big horse around the barrels.

My heart fell into my stomach. I wanted to go in there and pull her off that damn monster. Is this what she did in Montana? Did she ride the rodeo? I remember I asked her what she did when we were together those three days. She said she was a rodeo star. Now I listened to the speaker and the people. They knew her, and they loved her. That's when I realized it was her horse she was on. After she finished the barrels, she stood on the back of her horse and rode around the arena.

She spotted me and smiled. I smiled back. This was her life before the girls came. Then she had to work at the restaurant. She was terrific. She was almost to us when she jumped into the seat. And then she got down and walked her horse to where we stood.

"You're fantastic. This is what you do? I remember you telling me you were a rodeo star."

"Mommy, that was so fun. Can you do it again?" The girls surrounded her then Blade was there with his arm around her. He bent his head and kissed her. I wanted to knock that smile off his face. Instead, I turned and walked away. It was time to think.

31

GILLY

"I can't believe he had that tattoo put on," Lucy said as she sipped her coffee. "Whatever possessed him to do that."

"His mom thinks he's afraid because he feels too much. It doesn't make sense to me. What do you think, Gilly?"

"If he doesn't make a move soon, you need to say you are going back to Wyoming and check the property to start building on it. Or something. What do you think, Lucy?"

"You don't want to take advice from me. I married two times trying to get Adam to open his eyes."

"I think I'm not going to keep dating Blade. I think he's starting to like me."

"I wondered about that. I saw how he was looking at you, and it wasn't the look of a friend. It was the look of a man hot for you."

"Yes, that's what I was also thinking. So I told him last night that I won't be going out with him anymore. He said anytime I changed my mind, let him know. They say he's lethal; I have only seen gentleness from him."

"I know what you should do," I said. "You should act like

you don't give a damn. Treat Mace like he is just the girls' daddy, and that's it. Come to dinner tonight, both of you. Bring the kids. You can bring Adam with you, Lucy. You can even bring Mace with you, Hannah."

"I'm not sure I want to bring Mace. He'll think I'm asking him out. But the girls and I will be there. So how is the plumbing work coming along?"

The guy we hired is doing a great job. He has two others who work with him. So it's moving along. For now, we are still in Gray's home. Joe is at the Victorian keeping an eye on everything.

∼

"I WONDER where Hannah and the girls are? I'm calling Mace to see if he knows where she is," I told Gray and the others.

"Hello, Gilly. What can I do for you?" I could tell Mace was still angry at me for yelling at him over that damn tattoo.

"Hannah and the girls were coming for dinner, and she hasn't shown up. You know Hannah would have called me. Do you know if she's left yet?"

"I saw the girls over at Mom's a moment ago. Let me check to see where she is... Mom," I heard him call out.

"Grandma went to bingo."

"Where is mommy?"

"I don't know." I could hear their conversation. I could hear Mace's breathing change. He must be worried.

"Hannah, sweetheart, what happened? Gilly, call an ambulance! Hurry. She's burning up. I can't wake her up."

"I'll meet you at the hospital."

"I'm calling Mom to stay with the girls."

MACE

"What do you think it is?" I asked Craig the fireman.

"Mace, you've asked three times. Where the hell is the ambulance?"

That's when we heard it pull into the driveway. My Mom was right behind it. She started to cry when she saw Hannah. I picked Hannah up and carried her to the ambulance.

I was in the waiting room with Gilly and Gray when Lucy showed up. "It was her appendix. They burst, and she now has infection throughout her body. They are trying to get her fever down. I don't know how long her body will last if they can't get the fever down."

"Where is she?"

"She's in ICU. Do you want to see her?"

"Hell yes, I want to see her. This is why I can't fall in love. I can't lose her." I knew I was rambling but I didn't care. When I saw her lying on that bed, I tripped. I almost fell to my knees, and then I did fall to my knees. I prayed to God to please save Hannah. I begged him to take me and let Hannah live. I promised him everything I could think of if he would only save her life. All this time, I talked out loud and didn't care what anyone thought.

I got up and sat in the chair. Lucy left me alone with Hannah. "Sweetheart, please wake up. I have something important to tell you. I love you more than anything in this world. You and the girls are all I ever need. You are my life, baby.

"Please wake up and tell me you accept my apology for treating you like I have. That night at the Marriott scared the hell out of me. I knew that night that the love I felt for you was powerful. I thought me loving you so much would make something bad happen. I knew I could never go on if something happened to you."

I sat there with her for hours as the doctors and nurses came and went. Two days passed and I still hadn't slept. I was afraid if I went to sleep she would die, so I promised her I wouldn't go to sleep. All that time, I talked to her. I told her about my boys and Monica. I didn't even care the people in the ICU heard every word I said. I talked and I talked. The nurse brought me another bottle of water.

I went to the bathroom to wet my face and when I came back, the nurse and the doctor were there whispering. My legs buckled, I barely caught myself.

"Mace, her fever is going down. She's going to be okay." I nodded and sat down in the chair.

32

GRAY

I watched my wife and her sister decorate the tables. They were everywhere through the gardens at the pink Victorian home. Who knew the grounds would be beautiful once all the weeds were cleaned out? Today was Hannah and Mace's wedding. When Hannah woke up, she told Mace she heard every word he said and there was no way he was taking any of it back.

Mace didn't want to take it back. He wanted to get married right there in the hospital. His mom said they would have a wedding when Hannah got out of the hospital, not before then. So, of course, Gilly and Lucy decided right then to have the gardens cleaned and they set everything up.

Hannah cried, seeing how much work they did for her. "We didn't do the work," Gilly said, "we hired someone to do it for us."

"Same thing," Hannah declared. Now they were all ready to get married. The girls were dressed in pretty matching dresses. My beautiful wife walked up and put her arms around me.

"You make me happy, husband."

"Why is that?"

"Because I know you will be a wonderful daddy."

"When do you think we should have a baby?"

"I would say in about six months."

"What? I picked her up so our faces were even. Are you saying we are having a baby?"

"Yes, we are having our first child." She wiped her eyes as I kissed her all over her face.

Before we knew it, our friends and family congratulated us. I raised my head and saw Blade. He shook my hand. "You're staying for the wedding, aren't you?"

"No, this is one I will have to miss," he said as he walked away. I wondered if he had fallen in love with Hannah. Gilly wrapped both arms around me.

"The best day of my life was when you picked up the wrong date."

"Mine too, sweetheart," I said, kissing my wife with the beautiful green eyes.

THE END

Here is a look at MY NEXT BOOK IN Seal Security

This is about Hutch and Beatrice.
A LOOK AT HUTCH CAMPBELL

I stopped and looked around. I'm a Navy Seal. My heart was soaring; I was so damn thrilled. I looked at my buddies.

We all graduated together: Leo Hudson, Mace Cohen, Blade Wilder, and Hutch Campbell. We grew up together and knew what we wanted to do after graduating college. My brother Gray wants to join when he gets out of college in two years. But my mom is throwing a fit.

We worked our asses off to become Navy Seals, and tonight we planned on celebrating. The women loved the Navy Seal officers, and I planned to enjoy a certain woman with long black hair I saw working at the club last night. I'm sure she would love to be with a new Seal graduate. I didn't know her name, but I would learn what it was tonight.

"Hey, Hutch, are you going to stand there daydreaming, or are we going to party?"

"We are going to party all night. I'll call an Uber." I looked at my brother. "Gray, are you going with us?"

"Only if you tell the ladies I'm your Lieutenant."

"You got it, Lieutenant. Don't say anything when I take off with a particular lady server.

"Hey, who am I to say anything? But don't be surprised if I happen to find myself, someone."

"Don't piss me off, little brother. You are not leaving with a strange woman."

"What are you talking about? Grandma always tries to set me up with strange women I don't know."

"Yes, but she knows them. Let me warn you, from experience, don't go out with any of the women grandma wants you to. She set me up with Beatrice Price. I couldn't believe it when I saw her at the restaurant. We hate each other. We have since I was in the fifth grade, and she slammed the door shut on my fingers."

"Hutch, Bea felt terrible about that, and you know it. My God, she was in the third grade. She apologized to you so many times. Why have you held it against her for so long?"

"She laughed. She laughed at me when I turned around to see who slammed the door."

"I doubt she was laughing at you. She's not that kind of person. Bea Price is lovely. She's kind, and she would help anyone in need. You two were friends. I felt terrible for her because I could tell she had been sad for years. She didn't say anything about being sad, but I could tell she was."

"Then you go out with her."

"I asked her out she refused."

"You asked Bea out on a date?"

"Yes. Why not? She's terrific."

"Let's not talk about Beatrice Price," I looked around to

see where the hot server was. Then I saw her across the room, waiting on some guys.

"I went out with her," Mace said as he handed us each a beer. I would have taken her out again, but I mentioned the incident, and she got angry. She said you were the biggest baby she had ever known. Then she got up and walked out of the restaurant."

"I can't believe you dated her. You knew how I felt about her. Why have you guys always called it the incident?"

"Because you never wanted to hear anything about it, you would start screaming like a baby."

"I didn't act like a baby. Besides, I'm lucky, I could use my fingers after that injury."

Gray, spit beer he laughed so hard. Oh, please, your hand hurt for two days. It's not like it lasted years."

"I agree with Gray. Not only is Bea nice, but she's also hotter than hell."

"I took a long drink of my beer. *I knew how hot Bea was. I've watched her for years. I knew she was away at college. She wanted to be a doctor*. Honestly, I don't know why I acted like that. I tried to tell her I wasn't mad anymore. She slugged me in the stomach. After that, I stopped talking to her. "Damn, we are here to party—no more about Beatrice."

"Are you guys talking about the incident?" Blade asked, sitting down.

"No, we are finished talking about that. I'm going to see when that beauty gets off work and see if she wants company for the night." I walked back to our table with a grin.

My brother smiled. "I take it she said yes. Is that safe? Screwing someone you don't know?"

"Shut the fuck up. You are not ruining my night." They busted out laughing. I knew they set me up for that one."

"I have to go," Mace said, killing his beer. "I'm meeting Cindy. We have our own celebration to do."

"See you in a couple of days."

BEATRICE PRICE

I kicked my shoes off and sat down. Damn, my feet hurt. Medical school was murder. I knew it would be hard. So I was prepared for everything they gave me. Working in the ER all night was stressful. When I become a full-fledged medical doctor, I will be a pediatrician. I couldn't wait to have my own practice.

I got back up. My break was over. I raised my head when the ambulance brought in a heart attack victim. When I walked into the cubical, I recognized the man immediately. This was Hutch's father. We worked on him for a long time. I looked over at Doctor Johnson. We went to school together. He was always with the Campbell brothers. My mind flashed to Hutch Campbell. I haven't spoken to him since I was in the third or fourth grade. I knew everything he's done with his life. I mean, he was the popular kid in school. Now he was a Navy Seal.

I went into the waiting room. Mrs. Campbell and Jenny Hutch's sister were crying. I sat down and quietly talked to them. I explained to them everything that was going on with

Mr. Campbell. I told them how bad the heart attack was and that they might want to call the boys to be with them.

I was still shocked when I walked into the hospital two days later and ran into Hutch Campbell. He was more handsome than I remembered. When I ran into him, my hand touched his chest. It was solid rock, and my hand burned. He must work out all the time. He looks harder than he used to if that's possible. He was always hard with me. I saw how he was with others, and he wasn't hard with them. He was nice. *You are not a child anymore, Bea. Your feelings can't get hurt, yeah, right?*

"Hutch, excuse me."

"Beatrice, are you my father's doctor?"

"No, I'm working in the emergency room. I wanted to see how your dad is doing?" *I'm too close. He smells so good. It wasn't safe for me to be this close. I forgot to tell you that I've secretly been in love with Hutch since I was in the third grade.* We used to be friends until I let the door to the gym go, and it slammed on his hand. Now here he was, frowning at me again.

"Why don't you tell us how he is? We can't get any information out of anyone else. So Beatrice, please spill the beans."

Hutch is the only one I know who calls me Beatrice, and I know he does it because he's still angry about that damn heavy door. I refused to let him bait me. I turned and looked at who else was in the room. Gray, and Jenny. Their mom was in the room with Mr. Campbell. I sat down next to Jenny and took her hand.

"Your Dad's heart is plum tuckered out. He won't be getting any better when he leaves the hospital. He might live a few months. But he won't recover from this heart attack. It was too much. It's his third attack and his biggest. So when he goes home, he needs to be kept comfortable. Do you have any questions?"

"I do."

I knew he was going to say something. I turned and looked at Hutch. "What do you want to know?"

"First, I wanted to tell you that I'm sorry I acted like a jerk to you for all these years. I was a stupid idiot. It wasn't your fault the door closed on my hand. You were a small child, and I was an ass. I'm sorry. When can Dad go home?"

I sat there in shock all these years later, and he finally tells me he was sorry for being so mean. I shook myself and wiped at a stupid tear that fell from my eye. "Probably tomorrow. You might want to hire a nurse to help him. He'll be able to get around, but if he has pressure on his heart, it could cause another attack. You don't want him to become breathless. That causes the heart to pump harder."

He nodded, and I looked at the others. Gray was watching his brother. I think he was surprised Hutch apologized to me. I know I was. "Okay then, I'll see you later." I got up and walked out of the room. Mr. Campbell went home two days later. I went about my business with a secret smile in my heart because Hutch was sorry for treating me the way he did. *I was pathetic.*

SEAL SECURITY
    Ryker
    My Book
    Lincoln
    My Book
    Ethan
    My Book
    LUCA
    My Book

ARMY RANGERS SPECIAL OPS
  KASH BOOK 1
  My Book

BAND OF NAVY SEALS

KILLIAN BOOK 1
  My Book

Join me on social media Follow me on BookBub
https://www.bookbub.com/profile/susie-mciver

Newsletter Sign Up http://bit.ly/SusieMcIver_Newsletter

Facebook Group: https://www.facebook.com/groups/Susie-McIverAuthor

https://www.susiemciver.com/

https://www.instagram.com/susiemciverauthor/

Printed in Great Britain
by Amazon